*"Come...** [...]*
said, h[...]

She looked first at the hand, [...] [...]
his eyes. She knew what the invitation meant,
she could read it in his gaze. But she had to
hear the words. She had to be sure.

'Why?" she asked softly.

"I think you know."

"I want to hear you say it."

His smile was slow and lazy. "Do you want it
in writing, Doctor?" The smile took the sting
out of the words.

"What would you do if I said yes?"

He reminded her of a lion as he walked toward her, deliberate and purposeful, a sleek,
golden jungle cat, king of his world, stalking
the victim. But she had never felt less like a
victim in her life. She felt vibrant and alive, full
of joy.

Dirk didn't stop until he was so close, she
could see the tiny scar on his jaw. He cupped
her face with his hands, lifting it so he could
look into her eyes. "I would say, 'Get me a piece
of paper.' "

She took a long, ragged breath. "Are you
sure?"

"I've learned some things about myself, Ellen.
I've discovered feelings that are too strong to be
denied. I have to have you—no matter the
consequences."

The words echoed in her heart. They were
her feelings, too. . . .

WHAT ARE *LOVESWEPT* ROMANCES?

They are stories of true romance and touching emotion. We believe those two very important ingredients are constants in our highly sensual and very believable stories in the *LOVESWEPT* line. Our goal is to give you, the reader, stories of consistently high quality that may sometimes make you laugh, sometimes make you cry, but are always fresh and creative and contain many delightful surprises within their pages.

Most romance fans read an enormous number of books. Those they truly love, they keep. Others may be traded with friends and soon forgotten. We hope that each *LOVESWEPT* romance will be a treasure—a "keeper." We will always try to publish

LOVE STORIES YOU'LL NEVER FORGET
BY AUTHORS YOU'LL ALWAYS REMEMBER

The Editors

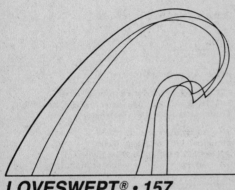

LOVESWEPT® • 157
Peggy Webb
Duplicity

 BANTAM BOOKS
TORONTO • NEW YORK • LONDON • SYDNEY • AUCKLAND

DUPLICITY

A Bantam Book / September 1986

Published simultaneously in the United States and Canada

---

*Bantam Books are published by Bantam Books, Inc. Its trade-
mark, consisting of the words "Bantam Books" and the por-
trayal of a rooster, is Registered in U.S. Patent and Trademark
Office and in other countries. Marca Registrada. Bantam
Books, Inc., 666 Fifth Avenue, New York, New York 10103.*

PRINTED IN THE UNITED STATES OF AMERICA

O   0 9 8 7 6 5 4 3 2 1

Because you taught me to love books, Mama,
this one's for you

One

"You're late." Dr. Ellen Stanford looked up from the notes she was studying and assessed the man standing in her doorway. He had the muscles of a linebacker, piercing black eyes, and a little-boy smile. She sighed. Trust Rachelle to pick a football player. "You're taller than I wanted, but you'll do." She set her notebook on a cluttered desk, perched on its edge, and crossed her legs. "Just so we have a clear understanding of this job from the outset, I am not paying you for sex—just to act as if we have it."

The man didn't bat an eyelash. He simply leaned against the door and surveyed her with those unsettling eyes. By the time he got to her face, she felt like squirming. Now she knew how all those poor bugs she had studied under the microscope had felt. She wondered if she should go back to Duke University and apologize to them. "Rachelle didn't tell me your name," she said. "What is it?"

"Dirk."

She liked his voice, deep and rumbly, like thunder in the mountains. "That's it? Just Dirk."

"Since we're not going to have sex, I think that's

all you need to know." His expression was as unreadable as Beech Mountain. Only the twinkle in his eyes betrayed his amusement. "You can supply the rest."

Ellen found her gaze wandering to his hips, noting the snug fit of his jeans, the powerful lines of his thighs. She almost blushed when she realized he was aware of where she was looking. Fortunately he didn't grin. If he had, she would have kicked him all the way down this North Carolina mountain, and she would have forgotten all about the family reunion. "I'll call you Smith," she said. "Easy to remember. You need to get acquainted with Gigi before we leave. She's out back waiting for her banana."

For the first time since he had entered the cabin, Dirk Benedict had second thoughts about going along with this charade. Somebody out back waiting for a banana sounded as if she would have all the appeal of his friend Anthony's snaggle-toothed cousin, Frances Jean. "Who's Gigi?" he asked.

"My gorilla." The good doctor slid off her desk with the nonchalance of a person who had just claimed ownership of a tabby cat. "She's waiting to meet you. Right through those double doors and to the left. My assistant, Ruth Ann, will show you the way." She turned her back on him in dismissal, picked up the half glasses she wore for reading, and began making rapid notations in the margin of the report she was studying.

Dirk gave her a final measuring look, adding the escaped red curl on the nape of her neck, the amber glint in her green eyes, and the graceful way she stood to his growing catalog of details. An extra burst of adrenaline pumped through his body as he shoved open the heavy doors and prepared to meet the gorilla. He chuckled to himself. For a man who had faced firing squads and assassins and some of the world's most powerful crime figures, one gorilla named Gigi should be a piece of cake. His overheated car radiator could wait. If that stunning woman in the white lab coat didn't find out his deception, this charade could prove to be just the thing he needed to take his mind off his work.

The minute Dirk was through the doors, Ellen breathed a sigh of relief. She was gifted with the power of total concentration, but right now her notes could not hold her attention. Why couldn't Rachelle have chosen somebody less imposing? she wondered. And why did that man have such a strong effect on her? She forced herself not to think about him, and to think about Gigi instead. The gorilla was making remarkable progress in the area of abstract thought. Although Ellen's work was labeled maverick and unsubstantiated by some of her colleagues, she believed that her methods of language research with gorillas would someday be the yardstick by which all other research was measured. She became so absorbed in her work that she didn't hear the front door open.

The young man, unsure of himself in the presence of a woman doctor, shifted from one foot to the other, and finally worked up enough courage to interrupt. "Ah, excuse me."

Ellen lowered her report and looked over the top of her glasses. She judged the sandy-haired, baby-faced man to be at least six years her junior, around twenty-three or so. "What can I do for you?" she asked. The transition from total absorption to charming hospitality was made so smoothly that the young man thought he had just dreamed that the doctor had been working when he'd come in out of the bright sunlight.

"I'm Nate Jones," he said, "and I guess you already know why I'm here." He ran a finger under his collar to release some of the sudden heat he felt in the presence of this awesomely beautiful woman.

"Why don't you refresh my memory?" Ellen suggested. She rapidly backtracked through her mind, trying to recall what her business with this ill-at-ease young man could be. Delivery boy for one of her suppliers? A new laundry man on the route? A reporter?

"It's about the—" He stopped speaking long enough to still the nervous bobbing of his Adam's apple. "Well, I need the money, you see, and when I heard about you wanting a man . . . That is . . ." He wiped the sweat off his forehead with a giant paisley print handkerchief. "Rachelle sent me." His snort of relief sounded like the blowing of a horse.

"Rachelle sent you?" Ellen spoke carefully, not believing what she had just heard.

"That's right, ma'am. I'm happy to go with you to the family reunion and pose as—"

He never got to finish his sentence. Ellen's notebook crashed to the floor as she bolted for the double doors. "Who the hell is that man back there with Gigi?"

Her feet flew down the corridor, out the back door of the building, and into the bright sunlit area that housed Gigi's summertime enclosure. She slowed down as she stepped into the sunlight and willed herself to regain her composure. Angry scenes were avoided in front of Gigi. Upsetting a two-hundred-pound gorilla could be dangerous.

She spotted them through the fence. Dirk and Gigi were sitting cross-legged, facing each other and sharing a banana. Ellen quietly let herself through the gate and approached the pair. She smiled in spite of her recent news. They looked like two solemn Buddhas, watching each other chew and pausing between bites for Gigi's ritual of carefully measuring and doling out the next two pieces.

Ellen sat beside Gigi and faced the man who called himself Dirk. "Who are you?" she asked.

"Found me out already, have you?"

"Yes. The man I thought you were is standing in my office right now adjusting his Adam's apple."

"The sex part made him nervous, did it?"

"You seem to have a one-track mind."

"This game was your idea, not mine." He stopped talking long enough to take the piece of banana Gigi handed him, pop it into his mouth, and solemnly submit to the gorilla's investigation to see if he was actually chewing. "I like Gigi," he said. "She's a woman of few words, Dr. Stanford."

"Five hundred to be exact. How did you know my name?"

"Your assistant, Ruth Ann. But seeing Gigi jogged my memory. I've read about your work. Congratulations. You seem to have done everything you claim."

"I wish my colleagues would say that! But let's not get sidetracked from the main issue here. You are not who you claim."

He laughed. "Maybe not, but you've already told me that I'll do. Why don't you fill me in on the details. Just what is it that you want me to do . . . except act as though we make love three times a day?"

"I didn't say that!"

"You disappoint me, Dr. Stanford. Only twice a day?"

"How often I make love is none of your business." She felt the blood rush to her face. She had never encountered a man who could keep her continually off-balance. What made it even worse was that she liked him. In spite of his deception, in spite of his word games, she liked the big hunk. She liked the way he smiled. She liked his unruly thatch of dark hair, his black eyes. She liked his self-confidence, almost arrogance, and the quiet dignity he used with Gigi. "The charade is over," she said. "You can take your bite of banana and go. The man I need is waiting in my office."

"How do you know I'm not the man you need?"

She chose to ignore the implications of his question. "You're too forward. You're too tall. You're too dark and you talk like a Yankee. Need I say more?"

"Yes. Go back to 'You're too dark and you talk like a Yankee.' Personal prejudices?"

"Partially. I prefer my men blond. As for the speech, my relatives are suspicious of anybody who doesn't talk with a Southern drawl."

"Once they get to know the lovable me underneath this Yankee exterior, they'll change their minds. But don't ask me to bleach my hair. There I draw the line." He winked at Ellen and shook his head at Gigi's offer of another bite.

Ellen stood up. "Tell Gigi good-bye. You won't be going with us to the family reunion."

Before Dirk could reply, Gigi grabbed him with one hand and frantically signed to Ellen with the other.

Ellen shook her head at the gorilla. "No, Gigi," she said while signing. "Man go. Ellen come back."

Dirk laughed. "I can't read what she's signing. American Sign Language, isn't it? But it looks like I have a two-hundred-pound gorilla on my side."

"Don't look so smug. You not only have her on your side, you're stuck with her. She told me, 'Man stay. Gigi love.' It looks as if you've made at least one conquest today."

"Just my luck. It's with the wrong woman."

Ellen laughed. "Don't let Gigi hear you say that. She's liable to take exception."

"You think she understands?" Dirk was genuinely interested. Ellen's work intrigued him, and he admired her courage in trying unusual methods of research more than he admired her legs. Which was quite a lot of admiration, he thought, for he hadn't seen a set of legs like hers since he left Paris.

"At least some of what we're saying," she said. "Probably more than we realize." She turned back to the gorilla. "Man like Gigi too. Man must go. Tell good-bye."

Gigi reacted to that outrageous suggestion by going into a corner to pout.

"This way, Dirk." Ellen preceded him through the gate.

"I hate to go and break her heart this way."

"Don't flatter yourself. I'll have Ruth Ann bring her some potato chips. She'll have forgotten you by the time she's ripped open the bag."

"Fickle woman."

When they returned to her office, the nervous young man was still waiting, standing beside the door and twisting his handkerchief into knots.

Dirk smiled as he lounged carelessly against Ellen's desk. He was going to enjoy this scene, he decided.

"I'm so sorry to keep you waiting," Ellen said. "What did you say your name was?" She noted the adoring-puppy look on the man's face and felt an instant sympathy for him. She didn't mean to generate that kind of adoration. It just seemed to happen.

"It's Nate, ma'am. I already told you once."

"So you did, Nate. My mind was on my gorilla."

Dirk noticed the way Nate's eyes widened at the mention of that fearsome animal. "The gorilla who's going with you to this family reunion," he said. Although he wasn't absolutely certain that was true, he thought it was highly probable. He had been putting together random bits of information. Anyhow, the statement was made to achieve maximum effect. He noted with satisfaction that it did. As Nate wiped his face with the most godawful handkerchief Dirk had ever seen, he could tell that the young man hadn't expected a gorilla to be a part of the deal. Dirk winked at Ellen, and thought that if looks could kill, he would be dead on the spot.

"A baby gorilla?" Nate asked.

"Full grown," Dirk said before Ellen could answer. "Over two hundred pounds. If I were you, I'd meet her before I started on a long trip. She might not like you."

"Rachelle didn't mention a gorilla, ma'am."

"Now don't you worry about a thing, Nate," Ellen said. "Gigi is harmless as a flea. And anyhow, my assistant is going along to take care of her." To Dirk she hissed, "You stay out of this."

"Excuse me, ma'am, but I'd like to get all this straight. I'm supposed to pose as your fiancé for all your kinfolks, and the gorilla is going too?"

Before Ellen could reply, Dirk spoke. "In the same car. Breathing down your neck, no doubt."

Ellen calmly moved closer to Dirk and ground her shoe into his foot. "Don't mind a thing my . . . cousin says. He's just jealous because I'm not taking him. But if you're a little nervous about this deal, I'll add another fifty dollars to your pay."

"Take it, boy," Dirk said. "You'll earn it." He slipped his arm around Ellen's shoulder. Ignoring her look of outrage, he squeezed. "My cousin here expects you to make love four times a day."

She scowled at him. "Whatever happened to three?" She was so furious that all her thoughts were focused on the audacious man at her side.

Dirk smiled and tightened his hold. "Was it just three, darling?" He winked at Nate. "A regular hell-cat, she is."

Ellen twisted out of his grasp. "I must apologize for his boorish behavior," she said to Nate. "Besides being unmannerly, he's a pathological liar. We're going to get treatment for him."

"Touché, Doctor," Dirk whispered.

She grandly ignored him. "Why don't we go outside so that we can talk in private, Nate? There's really no cause for alarm here. You can make friends with Gigi and—"

Nate interrupted her. "If you don't mind, ma'am, I think I'll just tell Rachelle I can't go tomorrow. It's not that I don't like you or anything. It's just that I don't cotton to the idea of riding in the same car with a gorilla."

"I understand, Nate," she said. "Many people would feel that way. I'm afraid gorillas have earned a reputation they don't deserve." She escorted him to the door. "I'm sorry you had to drive all the way up Beech Mountain for nothing."

Nate had begun to relax a little under Ellen's reassurances, but his Adam's apple still bobbed nervously from just being this close to a woman who looked as if she ought to be in the movies. "It wasn't for nothing, ma'am. It was worth the trip just to see you." He ducked his head awkwardly and walked out the door.

"That's one smart boy," Dirk said. "I think I'll see him out." He was through the door before Ellen could say a word.

Dirk caught up with Nate under a pine tree. "Thanks for being a sport back there, Nate. Sometimes that woman makes me lose my head."

"That woman, sir? I thought she was your cousin."

"I just met her today. I made all that up so you would leave and I could go on this trip with her." Dirk offered his hand and smiled. "No hard feelings?"

Nate hesitated, then stuck out his large, bony hand. "Can't say as I blame you."

Dirk reached into his pocket and pulled out a roll of bills. He peeled off two and handed them to Nate. "For your trouble. Take your girl out to dinner, on me." He winked. "We'll keep this between us."

"Right, sir." Nate gave him a glad-this-is-over grin and ambled to his car.

Dirk watched the dust settle after Nate had driven away, then threw back his head and roared with laughter. The hearty sound of satisfaction startled the squirrels in the pines and sent a covey of quail into flight. He had never felt so alive, Dirk thought. And he knew that it all had to do with a red-haired doctor and a gorilla named Gigi.

He turned and walked back toward the cabin when he heard the door bang open. Ellen was standing on the front porch with her arms folded across her chest. "You think this is all pretty funny, don't you?" she asked.

"It served the purpose."

"Well, why don't you fill me in on the details, Mr. Dirk Smith, or whatever your name is. You've ruined my plans, and I think I deserve an explanation."

His eyes caught and held hers as he mounted the porch steps. "The purpose, my darling, is to go with you to this family reunion." He leaned against the unfinished cedar post and gave her a beguiling smile. "You see, I'm just a lonely little orphan child. I've never been to a family gathering. When I saw this remarkable opportunity, I grabbed it."

"That's a likely story. You haven't told the truth since you set foot in my compound." The way his black eyes kept staring at her—seeming to see right through her, seeming even to read her thoughts—almost made her blush. What if he guessed that she had derived a strange kind of thrill from his touch? What if he knew that the way he looked at her made her want to run her hands through his hair? What if he guessed that her anger was partly real but mostly bluff? "And don't call me your darling," she added as that unrelenting stare unnerved her even more.

"I'm just practicing. I want to put on a convincing show for your relatives."

"Save your energy. You're not going. Rachelle can send somebody else."

"I'm not sure I'd trust Rachelle's judgment if I were you. She didn't do too well with Nate What's-his-name. If I were you, I'd find my own fiancé."

"I don't have time for men." She said it before she thought. This presumptuous man already knew too much about her. She kept giving him inches, and he kept taking miles. She wondered why in the world she had ever thought she liked him. He had to be the world's all-time champion arrogant horse's behind. And that made her the world's all-time chump for being sexually attracted to him. Just one set of genes calling to another was her scientific conclusion.

One dark eyebrow arched over one piercing black eye. "Tsk, tsk, my darling. All that sexual repression is bad for you."

"You can take your opinions and hit the road."

For the first time since she had stepped outside she noticed the aging Mercedes parked on the side of the mountain. "Is that your car?"

"Alas. My ever-faithful Rocinante has foundered for lack of water."

"Don Quixote?" Some of the stiff anger left her body at his whimsical humor.

He bowed from the waist and smiled up at her. "At your service, ma'am. My specialty is rescuing damsels going to family reunions."

She had to giggle at his poor imitation of a Southern drawl. "So your car stalled and you came into my office for help, huh?"

"Close enough."

"And I just automatically assumed . . . Why didn't you correct my mistake?"

"I'm on vacation and had nothing else to do. Besides, I like intrigue."

"You're vacationing here? There's nothing this far back in Beech Mountain except my compound and Anthony Salinger's summer place."

"Tony's a friend of mine. He's offered me the use of his cabin while he's in Canada fishing."

Ellen knew that at least he was telling the truth on this score. Tony had told her about his trip the last time they had spoken. Two weeks ago, if she remembered correctly. Why hadn't he also told her about this outrageous man who would be invading the mountain? Unfolding her arms, she stepped back and nodded toward the front door. "Come inside and get Rocinante's water. Tony's cabin is just about three miles up the mountain. You should be able to make it without further mishap."

He reminded her of a storm as he pushed away from the cedar post and crossed the porch. She could feel the power of him, sense the thunder of his emotions and see the jagged lightning in his eyes. "I'll get the water later," he said. "First this."

Before she could utter a protest, he leaned down and captured her lips. It was a light kiss, an experimental testing that was over almost before it had begun. She stood there, stunned, as he casually leaned back against another post and smiled at her. Her hands clenched into fists, and she had to restrain herself from reaching up to touch her lips. For some insane reason the kiss had made her feel lonesome. "Why did you do that?" she asked quietly.

"Because I like you, Dr. Ellen Stanford." The smile widened. Ellen thought that when he smiled, he didn't look arrogant at all. He looked like a little boy who was looking forward to Christmas. "And because I'm practicing for tomorrow. What time do we leave?"

It took a few seconds for her to put her mind back in gear, and during that time she wondered how she had gotten into this mess in the first place. Pure cowardice, she decided. Abject fear of facing inquisitive, doting relatives who believed that at the ripe old age of twenty-nine she was tottering on the brink of spinsterhood and neglecting her duty to the Stanford bloodline. This year, at least, she wanted to enjoy the family reunion without having to fend off dozens of questions and defend her life as a dedicated career woman. Just this one time she wanted to mingle with her kin and be like everybody else, engaged or married, and looking forward to motherhood. Next year she would find the right words to tell them that she was content to be a woman who talked to monkeys.

She sighed. Next year was a long way off, and she had never been brave in front of Aunt Lollie and Uncle Vester. Besides that she had already written that she was bringing her fiancé. She looked at the man standing on her front porch, not only willing to go through with the deception, but apparently eager as well. What did she have to lose?

"We leave at eight," she said.

Two

Ellen was having second thoughts before Dirk and Rocinante had disappeared down the road. She didn't know diddly-squat about the man, and here she was planning to take him to middle Tennessee to meet her relatives. Regretting her folly, she marched back inside and called Rachelle. As she listened to the ringing of the phone she decided that she might still be able to pull out of this mess.

"Hello. Rachelle's Sport Boutique." Rachelle's voice was so cheerful, it almost made the receiver dance in Ellen's hand.

Ignoring the good cheer, Ellen got right to the point. "Why did I let you talk me into this?"

Rachelle knew immediately what she was talking about. "Because, my Cowardly Lion friend, you're afraid of displeasing that Stanford clan, and I thought it was a good way for you to meet somebody."

"Nate?" Ellen couldn't suppress her laughter.

"He was a last-ditch effort. You should have seen the two that got away. Real heartthrobs! One of them was a linebacker for the Dallas Cowboys, and the other was a ski instructor on Sugar Mountain.

Hold on a sec." The ringing of a cash register and the tinkle of the shop bell sounded over the phone. "Hi. I'm back," Rachelle said. "Somebody renting golf clubs. Why isn't Nate going? He came by the shop earlier. He looked like he had seen a creature from outer space."

"He did. Dirk What's-his-name."

"Did I miss something?"

"No. I'm just getting around to telling you. This arrogant stranger had car trouble outside the compound, and I mistook him for Nate. He didn't bother to correct me. Anyhow, to make a long story short, he told Nate about Gigi, and I told him we leave at eight."

"Wow! He must have made quite an impression!"

"He made no impression whatsoever."

"Is that why you sounded all breathless and gaga when you mentioned him!"

"Gaga? You sound like Gigi."

"And you're evading. I'll bet he was big and dark and domineering, and probably the best-looking thing since Tom Selleck."

"How did you know?"

"You admit it! Hold on while I mark this momentous occasion on my calendar. The dedicated Dr. Stanford finally notices something wearing pants!"

"I'm not *that* dedicated. I'm just not quite the social butterfly that you are. Anyhow, I didn't call to discuss my social life. Can you find somebody else to go with me?"

"You must think I'm rolling in men. Not that I would mind, of course. No, Ellen, I'm afraid all the good ones are booked up for the weekend. Unless you want to face the music alone, it looks like you'll have to take Dirk."

"A prospect worse than death."

"The man or the relatives?"

"Both."

Rachelle laughed. "Somehow you don't sound like a woman facing death. I can't wait to meet this man."

"Don't hold your breath. Dirk is just a necessary nuisance."

After her conversation with Rachelle, Ellen delved into her work, trying to put Dirk and the family reunion out of her mind. But she kept remembering little things about him—that devil-may-care smile, the penetrating power of his eyes—so that by the time she was ready for bed, he had become more than a necessary nuisance. He had become an invasion.

She walked out onto her front porch, hoping the tranquillity of nature would dispel her eerie sense of having been caught off-guard. She felt like a fort with its battlements down. Not even the sound of the night birds restored the quiet peace of her Beech Mountain compound. Giving a small half-salute to the evening, she turned on her heel and marched inside to arm herself for battle.

It was the smell of coffee that woke Ellen. She pushed the tumbled covers aside and sat straight up in bed. The clock on her bedside table said 7:30. Good grief, she thought as she bounded for her robe. She was late. Fortunately, Ruth Ann was already making breakfast.

Raking her fingers through her tousled hair, she headed for the kitchen.

"Good morning, sleepyhead," Dirk said, turning from the stove. He held a coffee cup in one hand and a spatula in the other. "I thought you said we leave at eight."

Ellen had intended to be angry about his high-handed invasion of her house, but when she saw the white ruffled bib apron tied high around his massive chest, she laughed. "You look ridiculous in my apron."

"I thought it gave me a debonair sort of charm." He turned back to the stove and flipped the eggs. "How do you like your eggs? Sunny-side up?" he asked over his shoulder.

"I never eat eggs." She walked past him to the refrigerator and tried not to notice the way he watched her. She deliberately turned her back to him as she opened the refrigerator door, but the skin on her neck prickled with the awareness of his gaze. "Who let you in and why are you in my kitchen?" she asked. Looking at the orange juice instead of him made it easier for her to sound businesslike and remote, but not much.

"I let myself in," he said.

"That seems to be a habit of yours."

"It saves time."

She kept her attention focused on the juice, but her hand shook a little as she poured it. What was there about this man, she wondered, that seemed to unnerve her?

"I hope I haven't hired a cat burglar to introduce to my relatives," she said as she set the juice back on the shelf.

He laughed. "I can be anybody you want me to be. Even a cat burglar if you like."

She felt rather foolish still standing with her back to him, but she would rather face a firing squad than turn around and look into those incredible black eyes. To save face she began to putter around in the refrigerator, rearranging the cheese and stacking the butter sticks. "Why don't you become a lawyer?" she asked. "I've already witnessed your fast-talking tactics."

"I have a lawyer friend who would take exception to that remark." The spatula clattered as he dropped it on the counter. "Are you going to join me for breakfast, or do you plan to spend the rest of the day squeezing that butter?" His arms circled her from behind as he removed the mutilated butter stick from her hands.

She felt as if a thousand firecrackers had exploded inside her as his chest pressed into her back and his hands carefully wiped away the butter that had oozed from its foil wrapper. "I can do that," she said. She tried to take the small dish towel from his hand, but she might as well have been a gnat swatting at an elephant.

"This is a part of my contract."

She wondered if he was deliberately pressing closer to her or if her imagination was working overtime. "What contract?"

"Ours. I provide the loving; you provide the lying."

She whirled in his arms and immediately wished she hadn't. She was eye level with a tiny crescent-shaped scar on his chin, and her nose was touching his neck. He smelled of honeysuckle-kissed breezes and early-morning dew and pungent pine needles. He felt as solid as her favorite lookout rock on Beech Mountain and as timeless as nature. She was almost overwhelmed as Dirk washed over her senses, and she leaned against him for a moment to pull herself together. The feeling that he was one with nature persisted, but it was not nature's tranquillity that she was feeling. It was nature's turbulence—the vital, pulsing side of it that frequently assaulted Beech Mountain with thunderbolts and jagged lightning; the awesome side of nature that often made a mockery of man's petty strivings and his puny attempts at civilization.

"Are you judging me for 'lying' to my family?" she asked when she could finally make herself speak. "If so, you can take off my apron and go back where you came from. I don't need you."

He tipped her chin up with one bronzed finger so that she was looking directly into his eyes. "I need *you*." He spoke with an intensity that left no doubt about his sincerity. "I need a fiancée and a family and an interlude of ordinariness, even if it's only make-believe." His fingers caressed her chin. "No, Ellen, I'm not judging you. I'm using you as much as you're using me. I think it will be a mutually satisfactory arrangement as long as there are no questions asked. I have my secrets and you can have yours."

She drew a shaky breath. "You forgot the gorilla."

Much to her relief he released her and walked to the table, taking a heaping plate of scrambled eggs with him. "How could I forget my hairy sweetheart? She's the main reason I'm going." They both knew his remark was a cover-up, but neither of them wanted to continue the dangerous direction of their conversation. Too much of the self had been revealed, and too many unexpected feelings had surfaced.

Dirk looked up from his plate. "Join me, Ellen. I hate eating alone."

"Is that why you invaded my kitchen?"

"You ask too many questions. Sit over here"—he patted the chair beside him—"so you can prepare me for this reunion." He was not being totally honest, and he knew it. He wanted her to sit beside him so that he could watch the sunlight in her hair. He wanted her there so that he could memorize the exact way her royal-blue silk robe hugged her breasts. He wanted her there for reasons he couldn't afford to admit, even to himself. Dr. Ellen Stanford was the kind of woman he could easily become involved with, and he knew he was skirting the edge of danger. But he and danger were constant companions. Just this once he was going to allow himself the luxury of *feeling*. He was going to take the next few days as a gift, and when the time came, he would turn and walk away.

With Dirk's presence filling the room, all of Ellen's senses were heightened. She was conscious of the sunlight's warmth coming through the window, of the sensuous feel of her silk robe, of the mingled smells of coffee and eggs. Telling herself it was her natural scientific powers of observation and had nothing in the world to do with the man sitting at her table, she joined Dirk and gave him a capsule history of her Stanford relatives.

"The Stanfords are mostly farmers," she said, "most of them still in middle Tennessee. They are firm believers in motherhood and apple pie and the flag, so if you have any liberal views, I'd suggest you keep them to yourself."

Dirk grinned. "You've hit the jackpot. I'm a die-hard conservative. Of course, I prefer cherry pie, but I won't tell a soul."

She liked his sense of humor. If he'd just keep his distance, perhaps this trip wouldn't be so hard after all, Ellen told herself. "We'll be staying with Uncle Vester and Aunt Lollie." Noticing the way he was waggling his eyebrows at her, she hastened to add, "Separate bedrooms, of course. Remember you're in the Bible Belt, where hanky-panky is not taken lightly."

"I didn't plan to, ma'am. I'm serious about my lovin'."

She had to giggle at his ridiculous drawl. "If you're planning to pass for Southern, forget it. The Stanfords would spot that fake drawl a mile away."

"Aw, gee whiz 'n' shucks, ma'am." His corny imitation of disappointment made her laugh even harder. "I don't want to be a Yankee lawyer. They might mistake me for a carpetbagger and shoot me."

Into all this merriment came Ruth Ann and Gigi. Seeing the man of her dreams, Gigi wasted no time in shuffling across the kitchen and giving Dirk a gorilla kiss. Then she proceeded to hover over him and inspect his hair.

Dirk gave Ellen a lopsided grin. "What did I do to deserve all this?"

"You're the one who wanted to play the game."

Ruth Ann's eyebrows shot up into her Mamie Eisenhower bangs at the look that passed between Ellen and the fake fiancé. "Gigi and I are all set," she said. "If you and your fiancé are ready, I think we should be going." The way she said *fiancé* with her narrow nose pinched and her tight little mouth pursed left no doubt how she felt about the deception. Ruth Ann was a dedicated scientist from the top of her gray hair to the tips of her sensible shoes. She lived by the credo All work never hurt anybody, and if it hadn't been for Ellen, the fiesty little woman—who was more vinegar than sugar—would have worked round the clock.

Ellen put her arm around the slightly stooped shoulders. "Slow down, Ruth Ann. We're not going to a fire. This is supposed to be a leisurely family visit."

"Humph. No sense letting grass grow under our feet." She shot Dirk another withering look. "Gigi's already asked a dozen times when she'll see her brothers and sisters."

His eyebrows shot up. "Her brothers and sisters?"

"Uncle Mac's children," Ellen explained. "She adores them. She understands the concept of family and since I'm the only mother she has ever known, she calls my relatives her brothers and sisters." She turned to Ruth Ann. "If you can get Gigi interested in something besides Dirk's hair, he can load the car while I change."

The gorilla had to be bribed to give up her careful inspection of Dirk's hair, and twenty minutes later the strange group was assembled beside Ellen's vintage Buick, discussing seating arrangements. "Ruth Ann and Gigi will ride in back," Ellen said, "and Dirk can sit up front with me."

Gigi took exception to that arrangement, and when Dirk slid into the front seat, she abandoned all her sophisticated language training in favor of a primitive temper tantrum. Her gorilla ravings sent a frightened rabbit back to his burrow and startled a quail from the underbrush.

Dirk shrugged and climbed into the backseat. "What can I say? I'm devastatingly charming."

Gigi climbed happily in beside him, and the travelers started their journey to middle Tennessee.

"I knew he'd be trouble," Ruth Ann mumbled to Ellen over the roar of the steadfast old Buick engine.

"Everything's going to be all right, Ruth Ann," Ellen assured her. "Besides, Gigi's old enough for a little harmless flirtation."

Ruth Ann crossed her arms on her chest and gazed out the window at the blue morning mists still clinging to Beech Mountain. "It's not Gigi I'm worried about."

Ellen decided to ignore that remark. She was determined that nothing would spoil this trip. Not

Ruth Ann's negative attitude, not Gigi's crazy infatuation, not even Dirk's disturbing presence. She was going to enjoy this family reunion, even if the effort killed her. Each year the journey home was at once a pleasure and a pain—the joy of rediscovering her roots and the sadness of seeing time's ravages on her past. The childhood haunts seemed to shrink with each successive pilgrimage, and remembered heroes took on the smudged tinge of reality. She knew that part of the changes were in herself and in the time and distance that lent perspective to her viewing, but each year she made the journey. The return to her past enriched her present and lent meaning to her future, and she would no more have neglected it than she would have forgotten how to breathe.

She eased the old Buick down the mountain road at a sedate pace, but after she had crossed the state line between North Carolina and Tennessee, she zoomed along at a hair-raising speed. In the backseat Gigi clapped her hands in delight and Dirk leaned forward with a bit of advice.

"If this thing doesn't have wings," he said, "I think you should slow down."

Ellen was too busy negotiating a curve to reply, so Ruth Ann furthered his education about traveling with a gorilla. "Gigi likes to go fast. We try to give her what she wants in matters like these."

Gigi was now bouncing with glee and signing frantically to Dirk.

He looked from the gorilla to the woman he had privately labeled an old sourpuss. "What did she say?"

Ruth Ann looked at him over the tops of her glasses. "She said, 'Car fly. Gigi love.' " The look she gave Dirk made him wonder if he had something dirty on his feet. He made a bet with himself that he would make her smile at him just once before this trip was over.

He turned to stare out the window at the blurred scenery and decided that traveling at the speed of light with a gorilla who loved him wasn't nearly as bad as being shot at by hired assassins. He smiled and sat back to enjoy the fireworks. They were sure to come. If he was correct, that blur behind the last bridge had been a patrol car. He winked at Gigi and she winked back. Knowing that primates are great imitators, he spent the next few minutes of grace playing Monkey See, Monkey Do with his hairy girlfriend.

"Do I hear a siren?" Ruth Ann asked, leaning toward Ellen.

"What?" Ellen yelled over the roar of the engine and the sucking of wind through the ill-fitting windows.

"Never mind. You'll know soon enough." Ruth Ann's lips tightened as she waited for the inevitable. It happened every year. Ellen usually managed to talk her way out of a ticket and most of the startled patrolmen who stopped her ended up making friends with Gigi.

"Is that a flashing red light?" Ellen asked.

Dirk leaned forward and said into her ear, "It wouldn't surprise me. He's been trying to catch you for the last five minutes."

"Well, why didn't you say so?" With a screeching of tires, Ellen pulled off the highway and rolled down her window, calmly awaiting her fate. "It happens every year," she said to Dirk. As the Tennessee state cop approached her car, she smiled charmingly. "Lovely morning, isn't it, Officer . . . Burke." She had scanned the name tag so quickly that her hesitation was barely noticeable.

Officer Burke was not impressed. "Let's see your driver's license, lady."

Since speaking to him on a name basis hadn't thawed the frozen hostility on his face, Ellen tried friendly admission of guilt. "I realize I was going fast, Officer Burke, but—"

He didn't allow her to finish. "Excuses don't cut any mustard with me. Crime don't pay, lady." Officer Burke bent over his pad and began to write.

Gigi chose that moment to enter the fray. Since Dirk was no longer playing with her, she decided that perhaps this new man would. Baring her teeth in a huge gorilla grin, she bounced on the seat and emitted her best come-play-with-me grunt.

Officer Burke nearly snapped his pencil in two. He stuck his head in Ellen's open window and peered into the backseat. "Great jumping Jehoshaphat!" His face turned a sickly shade of green when he saw the huge animal. "It's King Kong!"

"She's harmless, Officer Burke," Ellen said hastily. "I'm Dr. Ellen Stanford, and she's my student in animal-language research."

"Never heard of no animal-language research. She looks like an escapee from the Knoxville Zoo."

Gigi decided that the man didn't want to play the game, but that was all right for she had spotted his funny hat. Gigi loved hats. Playfully she reached out a long arm and relieved Officer Burke of his patrolman's cap.

His face changed from green to purple. "I'm going to have to write this up, lady."

"Her name is Dr. Ellen Stanford." Dirk spoke quietly from the backseat, but there was an edge of steel in his voice.

Officer Burke turned his attention to Dirk. "And who are you, the monkey's keeper?"

"You might say that. Could I have a word with you, Officer Burke?"

"Dirk." Ellen turned to protest that he need not become involved.

He put a hand on her shoulder. "Sit tight, Ellen. This will only take a minute."

Ellen and Ruth Ann watched from the car as Dirk took the patrolman aside and engaged him in earnest conversation. Gigi lost interest in both men as she busied herself with her new hat.

"What do you suppose Dirk's telling him?" Ruth Ann asked.

"Heaven only knows." Ellen saw the officer's face change from hostility to friendly interest. "That man seems to have a way with words."

"You could have handled the situation." Ruth Ann's nostrils were pinched as she spoke.

"I know," Ellen said, "but reinforcements are sometimes nice."

Dirk returned to the car with Officer Burke. The highway patrolman stuck his head in the window. "If you ever need help on one of these missions, Doctor, just call ahead for Officer Burke." He gave Gigi a smart salute. "You can keep the hat, Kong."

Ellen could hardly hold back her laughter as Officer Burke climbed into his car and drove away. "What did you say to him?" she asked Dirk.

"The truth. I told him that we were on an undercover mission and that detection or detention would have tragic consequences." He didn't bat an eyelash at his outrageous story.

Ellen laughed. "You have a funny notion of the truth. But it did effect a nice rescue."

Ruth Ann rolled her eyes. "I'm beginning to think that you two deserve each other."

Dirk leaned nonchalantly against his seat as

Ellen pulled the car back onto the highway and roared off.

"How do you like the job so far, Dirk?" she yelled over her shoulder.

"I haven't had this much fun since I was cornered by a Bengal tiger," he said.

Ellen thought he was kidding.

Three

The mountains changed to gentle rolling hills, and after a picnic on the banks of a river, Ruth Ann took the wheel. Although she set a more sedate pace than Ellen, conversation was still difficult over the whistle of the wind through windows that had long since come loose from their rubber gaskets.

Gigi napped all the way from the river to Powder Mill Hill, six miles east of Lawrenceburg, and Ellen took the time to prepare Dirk for what lay ahead. "Ruth Ann and Gigi will be staying with Uncle Mac, one of my dad's brothers."

"He's not the uncle you said we'd be staying with?" Dirk hung over the front seat so he wouldn't have to shout to be heard.

"No. We'll be with my Aunt Lollie and Uncle Vester, another of Dad's brothers. Gigi needs this time away from me. We try to give her family-type experiences away from the compound so that she doesn't become too dependent on me. Uncle Mac is the only one of my relatives who has facilities for Gigi, and besides that, she adores his children."

"Her brothers and sisters?"

"Yes." Ellen laughed. "Uncle Mac looks upon Gigi and Ruth Ann as a part of the family. He teaches psychology at Vanderbilt—one of the few of my relatives who isn't a farmer—and he looks forward to this visit as much as Gigi does. I concentrate mainly on her speech, and he's interested in her behavior."

"What's it like having such a large family?"

The question startled Ellen. She had expected him to ask about the reunion dinner or Aunt Lollie and Uncle Vester. "I love it," she said. "They're the source of my strength. You might say this is a pilgrimage for me."

"They say you can't go home again."

There was a faraway look in his eyes that tugged at her heart. " 'They' are crazy," she said. "It all depends on the route you take. Is there anything else you'd like to know about this reunion? We never did get around to a briefing."

"No. Surprise me. I like adventure." It was true, Dirk thought as they both settled back in their seats. He had always liked adventure. He smiled as he remembered the childhood escapade of Miss Clampett's bloomers, her own name for the voluminous cotton garment she used for underwear. Miss Clampett had confined him to his room for "impertinence," her catch-all word for a variety of misdeeds. Like any normal ten-year-old orphan, he used the time creatively—to plot revenge. Unfortunately for him, his revenge coincided with the day of Superintendent Hanover's visit. When Superintendent Hanover saw Miss Clampett's bloomers flapping from the flagpole, all hell broke loose. Dirk had been expelled from the Lost Hope Orphanage in Boston and sent to the Good Shepherd Orphanage in West Haven. Two things had made parting with his friends bearable—the old black and white television set at the new orphanage and Mystic seaport. Jonathan O'Grady, the director of the Good Shepherd, was a kind-hearted soul who shared his passion for whales by taking the orphans on annual visits to Mystic and who believed the best education about good and evil was provided by TV westerns. "Now, remember, little men," Dirk could almost hear him shouting, "the guys in the white hats always win. Good always triumphs over evil."

Dirk's smile was tinged with sadness. He wondered what poor old Jonathan would say if he knew how wrong he had been. Sometimes evil won, but thank heaven the guys in the white hats were still out there fighting. Perhaps that was one of the reasons he loved his job: He was one of the men in the white hats. Sometimes, though, the hat became heavy and the evil seemed to be a cancer that was spreading out of control, eating away the foundations of society.

He swung his gaze away from the green earth of Tennessee and back to Ellen. Her serene, beautiful profile was a balm to his weary soul. How he needed this quiet interlude, he thought. How he needed to touch base with family, the backbone of America, to give his work new meaning.

He leaned back, letting Ellen's beauty seep into his soul, and by the time the car had come to a halt at Uncle Mac's farmhouse, he knew the exact structure of her bones and the precise tilt of her nose. He had cataloged the texture of her skin and the full pout of her lips. The sweep of her eyelashes and the bit of amber in her green eyes were forever a part of his memory, and he knew that nothing less than brainwashing could ever erase them. For the first time since he had embarked upon this deception, he wondered if Dr. Ellen Stanford didn't pose more danger than he could handle.

* * *

Ellen's Uncle Mac turned out to be a handsome silver-haired man who looked every inch the college professor. He kissed his niece on the cheek and shook hands warmly with Dirk. His three preteen daughters surrounded Gigi, and his teenage son gave Ruth Ann a bear hug. It was the first time Dirk had ever seen her smile.

Uncle Mac escorted everybody into his kitchen and insisted they take time for tea and scones. Although he had been a widower for three years, his spotless home reflected tender loving care. The teatime was Dirk's first real experience with the leisurely pace of the South. Listening to the conversation between Ellen and her uncle, he almost believed that schedules were for folks without refinement and that clocks didn't exist. He sat back in his chair and enjoyed the experience.

After Ruth Ann and Gigi were happily settled, Dirk and Ellen drove down the lane to Uncle Vester's and Aunt Lollie's. Dirk stretched out luxuriously in the front seat.

"Not that I'm glad to be rid of Gigi, you understand," he said, "but I'm beginning to know how a bug under a microscope feels."

Ellen laughed appreciatively. "Gigi gave you a pretty thorough inspection, did she?"

"She can now verify that nothing is dwelling in my hair or my ears and that I have all my teeth and fingers." He relaxed against the car seat. "I hope the rest of your family is not that curious."

"They probably won't do anything except count your teeth."

"A ritual of some kind?"

"No. A farmer's technique for judging a good animal."

Without cracking a smile, Dirk reached across the seat and ran his hand down the length of Ellen's thigh. His touch sent little prickles of heat through her light cotton sundress and silk slip. She ran straight through a four-way stop sign and narrowly missed a tractor hauling a load of hay.

After a maddening eternity, he removed his hand and smiled. "My technique for judging a good animal."

"Touché." The word was almost a sigh. She didn't realize that she had been holding her breath until he took his hand away. Unconsciously she pressed down on the accelerator, speeding toward their destination, lessening the time she would have to spend alone with Dirk. As the gravel spewed up behind the ancient Buick, she had time to reflect that there were chinks in her armor and that Dirk had an uncanny knack for finding them.

"So this is your childhood home," he said. He swung his head around to look out across the farmlands, tilled to a loamy richness and burgeoning with young green soybean plants.

"Yes. Lawrence County, Tennessee. God's country."

He studied her closely, noticing the sparkle of her eyes, the way her lips curved into a half smile. A wave of lonesomeness swept over him, and for the first time in many years he felt a vast emptiness in himself, a huge void that should have been filled with family and a place to call his home. His past was littered with a series of overcrowded, underfunded orphanages scattered across the country. Home was wherever he happened to be at the time.

"I almost envy you," he said softly.

She turned to look at him. For a moment she caught a glimpse of vulnerability in his face, a softening of the lines etched deeply around his mouth and a distant look in his eyes, as if he were gazing into his past. And then the look was gone. Once more he assumed a devil-may-care nonchalance.

He made a sound that passed for laughter, but it was hollow, without mirth. "You'll learn not to take everything I say seriously," he said. "I'm just a deceiver along for the ride." He wondered how many more lies he would have to tell before this reunion was over. Letting himself feel was getting more and more dangerous, and it could well be a luxury that he couldn't afford. Lesson number one, he told himself. Feelings couldn't be controlled with weapons and karate.

"That's exactly what I want you to be," Ellen said. This time she kept her eyes on the road. It was best not to notice that he was human. Instructing herself to think of him as a part of this experiment, this Ellen-is-a-good-Stanford deception, she concentrated on getting to Uncle Vester's farm as fast as she could. Fortunately for her, the gravel roads were free of tractors and pickers and plows. Otherwise she would have smashed half the farm vehicles in this part of Lawrence County.

Several cows stopped chewing their cuds long enough to watch her perilous progress through the county, and a few farmers, familiar with the aging Buick, noted that the Stanford girl was back in town, the crazy one who'd gone off to take a highfalutin degree and ended up on a mountain somewhere in North Carolina talking to monkeys.

Uncle Vester and Aunt Lollie were sitting on their front porch, straining their eyes into the distance, when Ellen's car entered their lane. They watched it weave in and out among the hundred-year-old oak trees.

Uncle Vester shoved his glasses to the top of his

balding head. "She still drives just like her daddy, God rest his soul. Mark my words, Lollie: Someday she's gonna wrap herself around a tree just like Mike did."

"Hush that foolish talk, Vester. She's the spittin' image of dear departed Evelyn, and now that she's finally giving up that monkey business and settling down I don't want you to say a word about how she's lived on that mountain all those years, fiddling away her life when she should have been preserving the family name." Aunt Lollie adjusted her blue gingham apron around her vast bulk and hauled herself out of her rocking chair. The cane bottom creaked with relief and the old chair continued to rock long after Lollie had vacated it.

They stood on the porch, their faces wreathed in smiles, as Eilen parked beside a 1955 Chevrolet pickup and ran up the steps to greet them. She hugged Aunt Lollie first, pressing her cheek against the sparse gray hair. The pungent scent of cinnamon tickled her nose. Some things never change, she thought. Aunt Lollie still smelled like gingerbread. As she gathered Uncle Vester to her heart she noticed that he fit loosely into his faded overalls, a bag of bones held together by stringy muscle and fierce pride.

Dirk watched the greetings from the porch steps. A faint summer breeze stirred the humid air, and a mockingbird on a nearby mimosa tree scolded its mate. Around him the earth, still damp from an early morning shower, released its rich, black smell. Dirk had the sensation of being in the center of life itself, of feeling the pregnant pulse of the land and of witnessing the miracle of growth. He decided to blame his feelings on too much companionship with Gigi. Otherwise he might have headed down the lane and back toward freedom.

"And is this the young man you wrote us about?" Aunt Lollie asked. As Dirk came up the porch steps she captured his hand in her fat ones. "My, my, you're a fine, sturdy-looking man." Her faded blue eyes perused him from top to bottom. "Good strong legs, *fine* breadth of chest. You'll make good babies."

"I have all my teeth too." Dirk smiled good-naturedly to show that he was not in the least bothered by Aunt Lollie's remarks.

Uncle Vester hooted with laughter and pinched Ellen's cheek. "You took your time about it, young 'un, but I think you picked a winner. What'd you say his name is?"

"Dirk Smith," she said.

"Dirk Caldwell," Dirk said at the same time.

Ellen gave him a "Be Quiet" look. "His name is Dirk Smith Caldwell, Uncle Vester. The third."

"Come from a long line of Caldwells, do you, son?" Uncle Vester asked. "Well, I like that in a man. Carrying the family name and all. Ellen's been stuck off on that mountain for years now . . ."

"Ves-ter . . ." Aunt Lollie warned.

Uncle Vester took Dirk's arm and bustled down the steps to get the bags. "Show Ellen to the guest room, Lollie. We'll have a little talk while we unload the car." He winked at Dirk. "Man talk."

Before she went into the house with her aunt, Ellen took one last look to see how Dirk was handling this massive dose of family. She need not have worried. He and Uncle Vester were laughing together like two old cronies. He looked up from the car trunk and signaled okay. His smile was so mischievous, she decided that perhaps she should be worrying for herself. There was no telling what sort of fantasies Dirk was spinning for Uncle Vester.

The screen door popped behind them as she followed Aunt Lollie into the house. Air conditioning was considered a modern foolishness by her relatives. The ceiling fans—their one concession to comfort—did little to cool the humid air. By the time Ellen reached the top of the stairs, her dress was clinging damply to her skin.

"Well, here we are." Aunt Lollie flung open the door to a large bedroom. A massive armoire dominated one corner of the room, a four-poster bed the other.

Ellen sat on the edge of the bed and bounced up and down like a child. "You still have feather mattresses! I'm so glad." Memories of days gone by flooded her mind. She could almost hear winter winds outside the window and smell the popcorn. She could almost feel the sweaty-sticky bodies of her cousins as they cuddled together in the featherbed, perspiring from the mountain of quilts Aunt Lollie had piled on top of them to keep them warm. "Will Emmaline and Carol be coming?" she asked.

Tears sprang to Aunt Lollie's eyes as she thought of her two daughters. "Carol and her husband are off in Spain. Lord only knows when they'll get back. They gallivant all the time. Emmaline and her husband will take the other upstairs bedroom. I'll put little Eddie on the den sofa."

Ellen ticked off the rooms on her fingers as Aunt Lollie talked. If she was remembering correctly, every available sleeping space had been accounted for. "Do you still have Carol's sleeping bag? Dirk can use that."

Aunt Lollie tiptoed to the bedroom door and peered down the hall. Then, giving Ellen a conspiratorial smile, she shut the door and tiptoed back across the room. "I wanted to surprise you," she whispered. "Vester and I still remember what it was like to be young and in love. You might say that we're modern in matters like these."

Ellen's heart sank right down to her toes as she realized what Aunt Lollie was saying. "I'm sure Dirk won't mind a sleeping bag for this short stay," she said, almost desperately.

Aunt Lollie dismissed that foolish notion with a wave of her hands. "Nonsense, Ellen. What would dear departed Evelyn say if she knew I'd made her daughter's fiancé sleep on the floor? Besides that, you're not all that young anymore. It would please me and Vester no end to know that your first child had been conceived right here in Lawrence County. Right here on this featherbed." She patted the bed for emphasis. A soft feather worked loose from the old mattress and floated to the floor.

Ellen looked down at the feather and back at Aunt Lollie. What could she say? she wondered. That Dirk was not her fiancé and that she didn't even plan to sleep with him, let alone conceive anything with him? Of course not. She had made her bed, as the old saying went, and now she was going to have to lie in it. She gave Aunt Lollie a brave smile. *Lie* was certainly an appropriate word for what she was about to do.

"I knew I could count on you to think of everything, Aunt Lollie. I just can't tell you what this means to me!" She certainly couldn't, she said to herself. It meant sleepless nights and a foolish, runaway heart. It meant pretending to appear nonchalant and trying not to look when he pulled off his shirt. It meant sorely regretting this charade and wishing that she had never heard of Dirk. It meant hoping she would not invite him onto that featherbed to embark upon an affair that she knew would be more than casual, an affair that would threaten her carefully planned future and jeopardize her heart.

Aunt Lollie clapped her hands in delight. "We both just knew you'd be tickled pink. Now, you two freshen up"—she paused to wink broadly—"and I'll go downstairs to see about supper."

A loud clatter outside the door announced the arrival of the men with the bags. The two old conspirators wasted no time in leaving Ellen and Dirk to themselves. Winking at each other and exchanging significant grins, they made their departure.

Ellen waited until she could no longer hear their footsteps in the hallway. "They're about as subtle as a freight train," she said. Her damp dress clung to her legs as she paced the room. She waved her arms around for emphasis as she talked, and she was altogether a different woman from the ever-cool, always-in-charge Dr. Ellen Stanford, who did primate language research on Beech Mountain. "What in the world are we going to do about this mess?"

Dirk began to unbutton his shirt. "I don't know what you're going to do, but I'm going to take a bath. It's hotter than the Equator around here."

"Take a bath!"

"That's right, my darling." He removed his damp shirt and hung it over the back of a chair. "Care to join me?"

She wanted to tear his outrageous grin from his face. If the sight of that magnificent chest hadn't stopped her, she probably would have. "Stop calling me that, and don't you dare pull off your pants! You've got to help me think of a way out of this mess."

As he strolled across the room Ellen spotted a jagged scar on his back. It started high on his shoulder and angled downward. She sucked her breath in sharply, and for an instant she forgot the matter at hand.

Dirk chose that moment to turn around. He saw the look on her face, the questions in her eyes, and he knew it was the scar. Damn, he thought. Short of explaining the scar, which he could not do, the only way to make her forget was to make her mad. He grinned as he reached for his belt buckle and began unfastening it. "I think the arrangements here are great." He pushed open the bathroom door and finished goading her over the sound of running water. "Don't worry, darling," he called. "I thanked Uncle Vester properly."

His ploy worked.

"You knew before you came upstairs? That's why you were grinning like a cat eating persimmons." She marched into the bathroom, intent on making it perfectly clear what she thought of the arrangements.

Dirk was standing beside the tub in his shorts. "Did you decide to join me, my darling?"

She threw a bar of soap at him. He ducked and it landed with a plop in the water. Dr. Ellen Stanford propped her hands on her hips and glared at the outrageous man. "My aunt and uncle may be a couple of old romantics, but I'm not. I'm completely uninterested in anything except my career. Your being here is a result of temporary insanity on my part, so don't be getting any ideas."

He hooked his thumbs into the waistband of his shorts and grinned at her. "I'm not. Are you?"

She whirled and left the bathroom. Putting her hands to her hot face, she stood in the middle of the bedroom in a moment of indecision. In a burst of guilty hindsight she realized she had reacted like a blushing teenager instead of a worldly-wise adult. He must think she was out here panting for that mouth-watering body. Well, she'd show him that he was nothing more than a business arrangement.

Thrusting out her chin, she marched back into the bathroom. Droplets of water dotted the black hairs on his chest and arms and glistened on his bronzed skin. For a moment she forgot why she had come. When her tongue finally unglued itself from the roof of her dry mouth, she spoke. "This is my charade, Dirk, and we'll do it my way. If you get out of line just once, I'll let Gigi have you." Satisfied that she was again in charge, she started to the bathroom door. Then she added, "We'll take turns using the bed. Tonight's my night."

She was limp with relief when she reentered the bedroom. "You forgot to scrub my back," he called through the open door. She replied by slamming the door shut so hard, it vibrated on its hinges.

Ellen considered it a small miracle that they made it down the stairs to supper before she killed him. Not only had he shown no modesty in getting dressed, but he had acted as if he enjoyed the whole thing. Her own bath had been a nightmare. He had tootled in and out of the bathroom, whistling and retrieving first his shaving kit and then his shaving cream, remarking that she was better-looking than any roommate he ever had in the Army, but that personally he preferred women with bigger breasts.

She was breathless and flushed when they entered the formal dining room. Seeing her, Aunt Lollie stopped tossing the salad and beamed. "My, my," she said. "There's nothing like a cozy afternoon to put color into a girl's cheeks."

Dirk wrapped his arm around Ellen and kissed

her on the nape of the neck. "That's just what I told my darling before we left the bathtub."

Ellen jabbed his ribs. "I napped while he bathed. Just couldn't hold my eyes open after that long drive."

"Well, boy," Uncle Vester said, "sit down and tell us about yourself."

"I'm just dying to know how you two met," Aunt Lollie added.

"It was at a concert," Ellen said.

"It was at a football game," Dirk said at the same time.

"Well, which was it?" Uncle Vester asked.

Ellen smiled at him over the vegetable soup. "To tell you the truth I was so stunned the first time I met him, I don't remember what we were doing."

"But you remember later, don't you, darling?" Dirk asked. "The moonlight, the wine, the hay-loft." He knew she was equal to the occasion, otherwise he would have found another way to protect himself. That moment on the porch had been an epiphany for him, and he had known then that the only way to survive this family reunion and walk away unscathed afterward was to submerge his feelings. He'd play the role of devil-may-care adventurer—along for the ride and any pleasure he could get from her.

She swallowed the soup and glared at him. Reminding herself that she had wanted this cha-rade and that it was all for a good cause, she plunged full speed ahead. "That must have been that wretched Waylings girl, Dirk." She tried a pout and hoped she didn't look like she had stuffed her mouth with cotton. "You never took me to the hayloft."

"An oversight I shall try to remedy, my dear." He lifted his glass of iced tea in salute to her.

"You can use mine," Uncle Vester offered.

Aunt Lollie, who could talk about making babies and cozy afternoons in public, but who thought real nitty-gritty sex should be discussed in whispers, kicked her husband under the table. "You've had other girlfriends, Dirk?" Her tone was mildly disapproving. For her, real romance meant having a one-and-only.

"Never looked at another woman after I met Ellen, Aunt Lollie," he said. "The poor little ol' Waylings girl was jus' a friend." He leaned over and pinched Ellen's cheek. "You know how jealous women in love can be."

Ellen rolled her eyes at his choice of Southern phrasing. She pinched him back and whispered in his ear, "Your drawl stinks."

Uncle Vester and Aunt Lollie could spot a Yankee a mile away. The ridiculous attempt didn't fool them. Now that they had determined he was virile enough to help Ellen carry on the Stanford bloodline, they wanted to know his background. After all, he was staying at their house. If he had anything to be ashamed of, they'd want to know before the big dinner so they could collaborate on the proper story to tell the rest of the clan.

"What part of the country are you from?" Aunt Lollie asked. She hoped it was somewhere glamorous like New York, but Pennsylvania would do.

"Connecticut," Dirk said. It was partially true, he told himself. It was one of the many places he was from.

Connecticut didn't sound like much to Aunt Lollie, but she guessed she could glamorize it by telling Fronie it had whales. "I don't suppose you work in one of those places with whales, do you?" she asked.

Seeing that Aunt Lollie was enamored of whales, Dirk said, "Whale sighting is a hobby of mine."

"He's a lawyer, Aunt Lollie," Ellen said. Her conscience hurt her only a little. After all, she was making them happy. She tried not to think ahead to the time when she would have to undo her fiancé.

"A fancy criminal lawyer, I'll bet," Uncle Vester said. He was so excited he slurped his soup. He didn't give a damn about whales. Money was what interested him. It would be wonderful if his brother Mike's only daughter had snagged herself a rich husband after waiting until she was almost an old maid before she got married.

Dirk cheerfully supplied information for Uncle Vester's fantasy. "I don't like to brag, but I'm the best in the country at what I do. I've come up against some of world's biggest crime figures."

Uncle Vester pounded his fork on the table with glee. "Whipped them all, did you, boy? Put 'em right where they belong."

"You'd have been proud of the job I did on them." Dirk knew that the truth can sometimes be disguised as fiction, and he salved his conscience by telling himself that he was making two old people happy.

By the time they got to the roast beef, Uncle Vester and Aunt Lollie were suggesting that Dirk might someday run for President, what with his background in criminal law and whales, and Ellen had decided that if Dirk weren't such an arrogant bastard, he would be the most decent man she knew.

As they walked up the stairs to their bedroom she put her hand on his arm and looked up at him. "Thank you."

He gazed at her beautiful face and thought of the four-poster bed and the long night ahead. "Don't thank me yet."

Four

Ellen began arranging their separate beds the minute she walked through the bedroom door. Her shoes tapped smartly against the polished wooden floor as she walked to the closet and began taking down quilts. Out of the corner of her eye she noticed that Dirk was standing in front of the window, apparently intent on gazing at the moon-lit pasture behind the farmhouse. Who was he, she wondered, this enigmatic man who was outrageous and arrogant one minute and thoughtful the next? She flipped a quilt in the air and spread it on the floor. It was more than scientific curiosity that motivated her. It was more than the remembered feel of his hand on her leg. She was fascinated by Dirk the same way she was fascinated by the unrestrained violence of nature. And she could no more explain that than she could fly to the moon. She only knew that from the time she was a child, she had taken every opportunity to stand at the window and watch a thunderstorm. No hiding her face under the covers for Ellen Stanford. No covering her ears and shrieking in fear. She had reveled in the raw power of nature just as she was beginning to revel in the raw power of the black-eyed stranger who was to share her room.

She added two more quilts to the floor, trying to make his pallet as comfortable as possible. "So you're from Connecticut?" she said. She tried to make the question sound casual, small talk to fill the time.

"Sometimes." He didn't turn from the window. He seemed preoccupied with his own thoughts.

"What about other times?" She covered her interest by retrieving a feather pillow from the closet shelf and placing it on the pallet.

"Here and there."

Strike a big fat zero for place, she thought. She decided to try occupation. "You played the part of a criminal lawyer quite convincingly, I thought. Is that really your profession?"

He turned from the window and gave her a slow, lazy smile. She shivered as if she had suddenly caught the attention of a big black panther. "Gathering scientific data, Dr. Stanford?"

She would have walked over hot coals before admitting that her interest was personal. "You could call it that. I'm trying to see if I can use you as an income-tax deduction. Research or legal advice."

"How about hanky-panky?" He crossed the room with long, swift strides and took her into his arms. "I believe that's what you're paying me for." His embrace tightened and he bent his head to nuzzle her neck.

She tried to squirm away, but not because she didn't like his touch. No, indeed. The problem was that she liked it too much. She liked the feel of his hot breath on her skin. She loved the way parts of her seemed to melt and flow into his body. She loved the hardness of him, the rocklike strength.

She liked it so much that a certain gorilla named Gigi was completely wiped from her mind. Years of meticulous research dwindled to nothing in the overpowering presence of this mysterious man. There was no room in Ellen's life for a man like that, a man who edged her work out of first place.

"Don't waste your performances on me," she said. "Save them for my relatives."

"This is no performance." He took her lips with embarrassing ease, moving ever so slowly, teasing, probing until he had elicited the proper response. She felt as if jagged lightning was suddenly coursing through her body. Her arms wrapped involuntarily around his neck, and she pressed close to his muscled strength as her lips invited him to further exploration.

There was a groan, a combined sound of agony and ecstasy, and neither of them knew who had made it. They were too enraptured by the thrust of tongue against tongue, the straining of flesh against flesh, the exchange of thunderbolt sensations.

A dozen thoughts hovered around the edge of Ellen's mind, seeking admittance, but she refused to allow them in. She knew that she was flirting with danger, but for the moment she was going to enjoy the excitement that only Dirk could give her. She was going to allow herself this forbidden pleasure, and then she would pull away and get on with the business of real life.

But she never got that chance. Dirk was the first to pull away. As she felt the ecstasy leave her lips, she opened her eyes and caught a glimpse of his face. It was twisted in lines of torment as if he were wrestling with demons more fierce than hers. He raked his hand through his hair, and strode quickly away from her. Was work his demon too?

she wondered. Or was it something else? What was the secret he was keeping from her?

Suddenly he whirled around, and his face was so untroubled, she thought she must have imagined his earlier torment. "I thought I'd get your mind off the questions," he said. "Did I?"

She clapped her hands together in mocking applause. "Bravo. You should get an Academy Award for your performance."

"The kiss?"

"No. The pretense." That she could move so smoothly from putty to iron was a tribute to her remarkable self-control. "You enjoyed that kiss every bit as much as I did. What are you hiding?"

"This," he said smoothly as he removed his shirt. He tossed it carelessly onto a chair. "And this." His hand moved to his belt buckle.

"Shock therapy won't work with me. Besides, I've already seen you without your clothes."

"Have you, my darling?" Giving her a wicked grin he let his pants drop to the floor. Hooking his hand into the waistband of his shorts, he said, "I sleep naked."

"I don't care how you sleep as long as you don't parade it around in front of me," she yelled. "You are the most conceited man on the face of the earth." She stalked toward the bathroom, muttering as she went. "Always talking about hankypanky and loving. Kissing me when I don't expect it. Lord, I should have stayed on Beech Mountain." She shut the door with a bang, and then opened it for one last word. "For your information, I've seen better bodies on gorillas."

To her heightened senses the movement of his shorts hitting the floor was like lightning. "Good night, love," he said. "If you get lonesome, just yell.

I'm right here." Giving her a last wicked grin, he lay down on the pallet and turned his back to her.

She ducked back inside the bathroom and leaned against the wash basin for support. What was the matter with her? she wondered. First she laid down the law about how this was just a business arrangement, and then she tried to find out who he was. Worse yet, she had come right out and told him that she enjoyed his kisses. Whatever had happened to the woman who did lonely research on a mountaintop, the woman who put her work first?

She splashed water onto her hot face and considered leaving Lawrence County first thing tomorrow. With water spiking her eyelashes and dripping off the end of her nose, she stood in the bathroom and weighed her options. On the one hand were the relatives and Gigi, happily anticipating the family reunion and her involvement. On the other hand was the audacious impostor in the next room, goading her with his teasing and his expert kisses. Leaving tomorrow would disappoint the people she loved most and would probably give that arrogant, no-name pretender all manner of perverse satisfaction.

She grabbed a washcloth and scrubbed viciously at her mouth, trying to wipe away the remnants of his kiss. How could she ever have thought she liked his kisses? she raged silently. Hell, she didn't even like *him*. She wouldn't leave tomorrow if Lawrence County sent out a posse to drive her away. She wouldn't give him the satisfaction.

Dirk knew by the way her bare feet slapped the wooden floor that she was still angry when she came back into the bedroom. That was just the way he wanted it, he told himself. He would use her anger to keep walls between them. If he felt a slight twinge of guilt at using her this way, he salved his conscience by telling himself that she was using him too.

He lay motionless on his makeshift bed and watched her walk across the room to the open window. The moonlight streaming in caught silver highlights in her blue robe and turned her hair to a fiery red halo. He loved the way she walked, purposeful and confident, yet completely feminine. He studied her lovely profile as she gazed out the window, and wondered what was running through that brilliant mind of hers. Was she thinking of her work? Her relatives? The deception? Was she perhaps thinking of him? The idea pleased him inordinately, and he wondered what it would be like to have someone think of him. Remember his birthday. Worry about him if he was late. Years of training in waiting stillness kept him from shaking his head in self-disgust. Who was he kidding? Men in his profession were automatically set apart from those things.

As she left the window and passed beside him, he caught a whiff of her perfume. It was like a breath of the outdoors, a light blending of wild flowers and heather, a scent reminiscent of spring showers and windswept hills. He reached up and captured her hand. "I was just teasing," he said softly.

The move didn't startle her at all. She had known he was awake. She had felt the pull of those black eyes as they observed her. She had sensed the turbulence of his emotions. She waited quietly, not saying anything.

"I don't prefer big-breasted women," he said. "I think yours are perfect."

"And I don't prefer blond men."

"Good night, Ellen."

"Good night, Dirk."

He held her hand a moment longer, feeling the surge of the current that snaked between them, and then he let her go.

She climbed into bed and sank down into the feather-stuffed mattress. But it was a long time before she went to sleep.

Ellen was up before the rooster crowed, but even so, Dirk was already gone. Out of habit she automatically began organizing her day. The first thing to do was get those covers off the floor before Aunt Lollie came upstairs.

She bent over the quilt, then stopped, her hand on the indention in the pillow where Dirk had laid his head. She stood with the pillow in her hand, staring into space. A sense of loss swept over her, a fleeting moment of regret for what might have been. Another place, another time, and things might have been different between them.

She came out of her reverie and finished gathering the quilts off the floor. She was not one to waste time in useless regrets or senseless pipe dreams. Besides, she heard the whooshing of Aunt Lollie's felt bedroom slippers in the hallway; her aunt wore the felt slippers the year round. Smiling, Ellen quickly deposited the quilts and pillow on the top shelf of the closet.

"Are you up, dear?" Aunt Lollie asked, sticking her head around the door. Seeing Ellen standing beside the closet, she bustled into the room. "Dirk's been up for ages. My, my, he's a regular country boy. Followed Vester to the barn just like he'd been doing it all his life." She puttered around as she talked, dusting the bedposts and rearranging the crocheted coverlet. "You'd think a man of his status, being familiar with whales and all, would be uppity. My, my. Not that boy. There's not an uppity bone in his body."

Aunt Lollie stopped talking long enough to give Ellen a keen look. "You look a mite peaked, dear. Didn't you sleep well?"

"I slept fine, Aunt Lollie. It's just that I'm not used to a featherbed." Or to sleeping in the same room with a man as unnerving as Dirk, she added to herself.

Aunt Lollie put her arm around Ellen. "I know what you need. A nice country breakfast. Put some color into your cheeks. I've never seen anything that couldn't be fixed with a big plate of ham and eggs."

Ellen smiled. Aunt Lollie loved to fix things, especially people's problems. If they didn't already have one, she'd invent it. "I never eat eggs, Aunt Lollie. You know that."

"Oh, pshaw! You need to pick up a little weight before the wedding. You're as skinny as a fence pole." She laughed. "You should have seen the breakfast that man of yours put away. A fine figure of a man, he is!"

She didn't know the half of it, Ellen thought. What would Aunt Lollie say if she could see Dirk without his clothes? The instant the thought came into her head, Ellen tried to dismiss it. What did it matter how he looked without his clothes, for Pete's sake? She quickly changed the subject.

"Speaking of skinny, Aunt Lollie, I'm worried about Uncle Vester. He seems to have lost a lot of weight this past year. Is anything wrong?"

"The doctor put him on one of those low-fat diets. I told the silly old poop if he didn't start eating again, he was going to dry up and blow away. Besides that, I said to him, 'How do you expect to ever get to Las Vegas if you don't have your strength?' He's been saving to go there for years. Personally I'd prefer to go up to Connecticut and see the whales. Dirk said he'd be glad to show them to me."

Ellen decided that she had created a monster. Instead of a short-term fiancé, Dirk had become a hero. When they weren't singing his praises, Aunt Lollie and Uncle Vester were quoting things he'd said. The next thing she knew, they'd be making plans to move to Connecticut.

As she began to dress, she made one last futile attempt to steer the subject away from Dirk. "Is there anything I can do to help you get ready for the reunion dinner?"

"All I want you to do is look as pretty as possible. I want to show you off. Not all the Stanford girls turned out as nice as you did. You're a fine-looking woman. Dirk thinks so too."

Ellen sighed. It was useless. She couldn't tell Aunt Lollie that she didn't care what Dirk did or said. And she certainly couldn't tell her that she didn't want to be shown off. Among the Stanford clan if you had anything to brag about you did, and if you had nothing to brag about, you invented something. It was an iron-clad rule, as unshakable as the Tennessee earth. Ellen resigned herself to being shown off. She quickly finished dressing and followed Aunt Lollie down the stairs to the kitchen.

Dirk was lounging casually against the back door, looking rugged and windswept and altogether too sexy. "Good morning, love," he said. Ellen's face grew flushed as he strolled across the floor and kissed her soundly on the mouth. "Sleep well?"

She could have shot him on the spot. He knew

damn well she hadn't slept well. But then, neither had he. She had heard every restless move he had made. A wicked grin played around her lips as she decided to give him a dose of his own medicine. "You should know," she said. "You're the one who kept insisting that we not let the featherbed go to waste, love." To Dirk's astonishment she leaned over and flicked her tongue in his ear.

His arm snaked around her waist, and he pulled her in tight to whisper in her ear. "Don't you think you're overacting a bit, my dear?"

"You're the one who started it," she whispered back.

Keeping his arm around her waist, he straightened up and spoke in a normal voice. "I've been exploring the farm this morning. It's a wonderful place."

Now that their little performance was over, Ellen discreetly tried to disengage his hand from her waist. She might as well have been wrestling with an octopus. She decided to let it go. At least he was making sensible conversation now. "The farm is wonderful, isn't it?" she said. "What part of it did you see this morning?"

"The hayloft." He grinned down at her. "It's the perfect spot for what I have in mind."

She smiled sweetly and ground down on his foot with the heel of her shoe. "It's perfect for what I have in mind too." Turning her face so that Aunt Lollie couldn't see, she rolled her eyes and mouthed at Dirk, "Murder."

He laughed.

Aunt Lollie, who had been avidly following their conversation, spoke up. "Now you children just run on." Smiling, she waved her apron at them. "Shoo. Go on outside and explore the farm while I fix Ellen's ham and eggs."

Ellen didn't want the ham and eggs, and she certainly didn't want to explore the farm with Dirk, but it would be pointless to tell Aunt Lollie so.

"Ring the bell when you want me, Aunt Lollie," she said. "I'll be at my favorite spot."

"Does Dirk know about your favorite spot?" Aunt Lollie asked.

"Not yet." Ellen grinned. "But he will."

"My, my," Aunt Lollie said as they walked out the door. "That girl's a sight."

The door banged shut behind them as they stepped out into the early-morning sunshine. Hearing the sound, a small black and tan beagle loped across the yard and flung himself at Ellen's feet. She and Dirk bent down at the same time, and their hands met on the small fuzzy head.

Casually Dirk began to caress the beagle's floppy ears, but there was nothing casual in the way he felt. It was odd, he mused, how the unexpected touch of Ellen's hand had suddenly made him feel vulnerable. It wasn't as if he had never touched her before. But there was something different this time. He guessed it had to do with the spontaneity of the touch, with the way they had reached toward the dog with affection. "A nice pet," he commented.

Ellen hadn't missed a thing: the way his face had changed when their hands touched, the way he had pulled back from the contact. She fondled the beagle's head. "Uncle Vester always has at least one dog on the farm. He says pets are God's way of making people feel good about themselves."

"That could be true. I never had a chance to find out."

She studied his face closely. She had the feeling that a lonely little boy was peeping through his eyes. "Why did you never have a chance?"

He was immediately on guard. "You don't believe in subtlety, do you?"

"No. Why do you always answer a question with a question?"

"Do I do that?" He gave the beagle one final pat and straightened. Life was deceptively simple on the farm, he thought. Feelings blossomed as naturally as the crops. The simple joy of petting a dog had set off a chain of feelings he had thought long buried. Childhood memories had tumbled out of hiding: of being six and having a child's faith that his stocking would be stuffed with a puppy, simply because he had written a letter to Santa; of being ten and falling in love with an old lop-eared stray hound that the orphanage director wouldn't let him keep; of being twelve and longing for something, even a goldfish, to call his own. If he wasn't careful, the door to that secret place where he kept his feelings would be wide open and he would have a hard time shutting it again.

She shook her head in mock exasperation. "I think you should know that I don't give up easily. I intend to use this walk to explore more than the farm."

Once more he assumed the mask of the reckless deceiver. "Why do I get the feeling that I've walked into a trap?" he asked.

She smiled up at him, enjoying the crisp morning air, enjoying the feel of the sun on her skin, even enjoying Dirk's company. "Do I look like the kind of woman who would lay a trap?"

"Yes."

"Then why did you come along?"

"Curiosity," he told her. Compulsion, he told himself. Excitement. Intrigue. He lived on the cutting edge of danger, and she was a new kind of danger, a challenge he had never before allowed himself to face.

"Curiosity killed the cat," she said.

"Don't you know that cats have nine lives?"

She smiled. "Don't say I didn't warn you." Spreading her arms wide as if to embrace the sun, she ran ahead of him across the pasture. Dew wet her shoes and honeysuckle drugged her senses. The man at her side was almost forgotten as she reentered the world of her childhood. Placid cows chewing their cud ignored her, and a family of martins was startled into flight by her exuberant progress across the pasture.

"Last one over the fence is a rotten egg," she called as she put her hand on the wire and vaulted over. She stopped long enough to watch the Yankee make a fool of himself on the barbed wire. She was going to enjoy this, she thought. It would serve him right for all those remarks about the hayloft.

Dirk was no stranger to barbed wire. He easily negotiated the fence.

"How did you do that?" she asked.

"It's one of my many talents." He smiled at her, a lazy cat's smile. "I'm especially talented in the hayloft. Would you like a demonstration?"

She stared at him, standing there with the sun turning his eyes to dark crystals. What would he do if she said yes? she wondered. What would he say if he knew that she had wanted a demonstration from the moment she saw him in her home on Beech Mountain? She would never know. She already felt too much for this man. Admiration. Strong attraction. Even compassion for the vulnerable little boy she had glimpsed beneath his surface arrogance. No, she reasoned, a turn in the hayloft would be more than a demonstration: It would be a beginning, a beginning that she had forbidden.

"No," she said rather stiffly.

"Another time, perhaps," he said softly.

"There will be no other time for us, Dirk."

The words hung between them like mists off Beech Mountain. He knew that what she was saying was true. Although he had made the hayloft offer halfway in jest, there was nothing frivolous in the way he felt. He supposed he should be grateful to her for putting up a stop sign. It was something that he should have done a long time ago.

"You're right," he said. "I keep forgetting that I'm just a hired fiancé." He turned and stepped back across the fence.

She didn't know what she had expected, but it certainly hadn't been such ready agreement. For some reason she was disappointed. "Aren't you going with me to my favorite place?" she asked.

"Not today." Not ever, he added to himself. Favorite places weren't allowed in his kind of work. He walked away and never looked back. He knew that if he looked back at her, he might change his mind.

Ellen squared her shoulders and lifted her chin. "Well, good riddance," she muttered, but she didn't mean it. She didn't mean it at all. She looked up at a mockingbird sitting on the topmost branch of an ancient oak tree. "What's the matter with me?" she asked.

The bird gave her no answer. She waited a moment, trying not to look at Dirk's departing back, and then she could stand it no longer. She turned and watched him walk back toward the farmhouse. His shoulders were squared and his gait was strong and determined, but there was no jauntiness in his step. Her heart lurched crazily and she wanted to run after him, but she remained on the other side of the fence. "This is where I belong," she told the bird.

Finally she made her way to her favorite place, but some of the magic was gone.

The Davy Crockett State Park was the site of the annual Stanford family reunion. Ellen parked her faithful Buick in the shade of a giant cottonwood tree and turned to her companions. "This is it, gang. Time for our big performance."

"Why do I feel like a Christian being thrown to the lions?" Dirk asked.

"Don't worry. Gigi will protect you."

He looked at the large black hand gripping his shoulder. "That's what worries me."

Ruth Ann sniffed. "No need to make a federal case out of a simple matter." Reaching into her large handbag, she brought out a package of potato chips. "Come with me, Gigi. We'll have a little snack before lunch."

Gigi didn't need sign language to tell her what was going on. The sight of the bag of chips was enough. She released Dirk and happily exited the car with Ruth Ann.

"Saved by Old Sourpuss," he said dryly.

"Don't let her looks fool you," Ellen said. "She has a heart of gold."

"And the suspicious nature of a hedgehog." He dismissed his nemesis with a laugh. "Let's get on with the show."

Ellen stepped from the car and somewhat self-consciously took Dirk's arm. The sun had passed its zenith and was beaming down on the reunion crowd with a vengeance. Oppressive heat was rising from the ground in waves, wilting the chattering, milling Stanfords and their various husbands, wives, in-laws, and children. Ellen sent a little prayer winging upward that the deception would work.

As she led Dirk toward the crowd she glanced up at him to see his first reaction to her relatives. His expression was cool and detached, telling her nothing. It had been like that since the incident beside the fence this morning. She wondered what he was thinking, then quickly decided that it didn't matter. Men with murky backgrounds and unknown professions didn't mix with women dedicated to lonely mountaintop research.

Suddenly she tensed, awaiting the fireworks as her great-aunt Hortense descended on them. Hortense had two claims to fame among the Stanfords: her razor tongue and her trumpet voice. She used both without mercy. A session with Aunt Hortense had been known to reduce the otherwise brave and hearty to a sniveling coward.

"So this is the fiancé," Aunt Hortense said. Her watery gray gaze swept over Dirk from head to toe, then she turned to Ellen. "Nobody told me he had black eyes. I never did trust a man with black eyes." Her loud condemnation of black-eyed men stemmed from personal experience. Her husband, a black-eyed, black-bearded giant of a man, had run off with another woman after fifteen years of wedded bondage to the formidable Hortense.

Ellen groaned silently. Why couldn't Dirk have met Aunt Gert or Uncle Henry first? Why couldn't it have been anybody except Aunt Hortense? "Dirk, meet Aunt Hortense Winfield. Aunt Hortense, Dirk Smith—" She stopped, horrified. She couldn't even remember what his name was supposed to be!

"Caldwell, the Third," he said smoothly. Bending

at the waist, he gallantly took Aunt Hortense's hand and lifted it to his lips. "You don't mind if I call you Aunt, too, do you?" He tucked her hand under his arm and began walking toward the covered pavilion. "Although I must say, you look much too young to be anybody's aunt." He checked the reaction to his flattery and saw the lines in her face soften. Poor old lady, he thought. Probably some dark-eyed man had abused her trust.

Ellen watched with amazement as the legendary Stanford battle-ax lost some of her cutting edges. She shouldn't be surprised, she told herself. She had lost some of her own edges since Dirk had come into her life. She walked beside them and continued to marvel as he charmed her aunt.

"What do you think about Robert E. Lee?" he asked Hortense.

"He's one of the South's finest men. The salt of the earth," Aunt Hortense said.

"And Jefferson Davis?" Dirk asked as they passed under a mimosa tree in full bloom.

"It was a great day for the South when that man was born."

"They were men worthy of trust, wouldn't you say?" Dirk went on.

"I would swear by Jefferson Davis and Robert E. Lee," Aunt Hortense vowed loudly.

Dirk's eyes twinkled. "They were black-eyed men."

Aunt Hortense's lace-up shoes skidded to a stop on the worn path. Dust whirled around them and settled in the pores of their skin. "Young man, are you casting slurs on the South?" Aunt Hortense drew herself up to her full height. She had always prided herself on being able to look a body—man or woman—straight in the eyes. But even stretching her neck and standing almost on tiptoe, she couldn't get eye level with Dirk.

"No, ma'am," he said, and Ellen cringed at his fake drawl. "I'm trying to make a case for black-eyed men."

Aunt Hortense was solemn as a judge as she stood in the dusty path and pondered Dirk's statement. Then she tipped her head back and roared with laughter. Tears of mirth rolled from her eyes, settling in her wrinkles so that her face looked like a road map. "I do declare." She whooped with joy. "Well, I do declare." Turning to Ellen she said, "Young woman, you've found yourself a treasure. A downright treasure. Any man who can stand up to this old battle-ax is worth hanging on to." She patted Dirk's cheek and left the two of them, shaking her head as she went. "Who would have ever thought . . . a black-eyed man!"

After Aunt Hortense had disappeared into the crowd, Ellen looked up at Dirk. "Did they really?"

He feigned innocence. "Did who really what?"

"Did Robert E. Lee and Jefferson Davis have black eyes?"

"How should I know? I'm a Yankee."

"You're a fake." But a charming one, she added to herself. Dangerously charming. He casually threw his arm across her shoulders, and she felt a heat that had nothing to do with the weather. "Who are you, Dirk Smith Caldwell the Third?"

"I'm the man you've created. Your fiancé. The man of your dreams." His arm tightened, and for a moment she thought he was going to bend down and kiss her.

She stood still, inhaling the too sweet fragrance of mimosa blossoms and looking into his eyes. An amber light shone briefly out of their depths, a spark of fire and tenderness that revealed the man

beneath the facade, and then they became unreadable again, shuttered and as black as doom. She
thought that she would never again smell mimosa
blossoms without remembering that light in his
eyes.

"Let's go, man of my dreams," she said lightly.
"We mustn't keep the Stanfords waiting."

Five

Ellen sat on the redwood bench, picking at her food and watching Dirk move among her relatives. She had to admit that he had done a wonderful job of playing her fiancé. He had charmed everybody from Aunt Hortense all the way down to the dreadful Wilcox twins. Glenda Wilcox, the only Stanford woman said to have married beneath herself, had remarked as she sat down with her plate of fried chicken that she'd give a million dollars—if she had it—to have a man like that around the house. The way she had batted her dime-store eyelashes, glued on crooked and looking like two bats on her face, it was obvious she had more in mind than baby-sitting. Ellen's smile was tender as she recalled how Dirk had made Glenda feel special without leading her on. He had that knack, she realized: making people feel special. That was just one of the growing list of things that Ellen liked about him.

Uncle Vester eased onto the bench beside her, his old knee joints popping as he sat down. "Yessir, hon," he said, "that boy's a treasure, as Lollie would say." He took a three-bladed knife from his pants pocket and began to shave golden kernels of corn off the cob onto his plate. "Even if he is a Yankee, I think you're marrying up."

Ellen laughed. Marrying up was the opposite of marrying beneath oneself. And marrying beneath oneself was the worst thing that could happen to a Stanford woman. Only the flighty, like Glenda, were so foolish. Of course, several of the Stanford women had been known to marry and become martyrs, but suffering imparted a dignity that foolishness did not. Ellen's smile took on a tinge of sadness as she thought of all the codes her relatives lived by. She was no longer a part of them, she thought. Even being here at the reunion, she felt worlds away.

Uncle Vester stopped shaving the corn and gave his niece a keen look. His gnarled hand covered hers. "What's the matter, hon? All of a sudden you look like you have a case of the lonesomes."

She squeezed his hand. Of all her father's brothers, and there were four of them, Uncle Vester understood her best. He didn't always agree with her life-style choices—Lord knows how many times he had fussed about her living on that mountain—but he was always sensitive to her moods. He could bluster and wink and brag with the best of the Stanfords, but deep down he only wanted Ellen to be happy.

"I guess I do," she admitted, "but I don't know why. I'm seeing cousins I haven't seen in years, aunts and uncles I haven't seen since last year . . ."

Uncle Vester interrupted her. "People don't have a thing to do with the lonesomes. It's a feeling that starts in the heart. It's a great old big empty place that will eat you up if you don't fill it with something."

Just at that moment Ellen heard Dirk's laughter. She lifted her head and looked at him across the pavilion. He was sitting beside her great-uncle Lloyd, the reigning patriarch of the Stanford family, and he looked so carefree, so genuine that she almost forgot he was playing out a deception. Was he the reason for her case of the lonesomes? she wondered. Was there an empty place in her heart that couldn't be filled by Gigi and the compound on Beech Mountain?

She made a small sound of denial, but it died on her lips as Dirk looked up and smiled at her across the heads of her relatives. It was an electric smile that hit her with a shock and seared its way into her heart. It was a smile of kinship, of one deceiver to another. And it was a smile that made her wonder if he, too, was suffering from a case of the lonesomes.

"Eat your corn before it gets cold, Uncle Vester," she said. "I think I'll try a piece of Aunt Fronie's chocolate cream pie."

It was Fronie's chocolate cream pie that started the whole thing. Renowned in Lawrence County for her cooking, Fronie was particularly famous for her cream pies. Her sister Lollie even admitted to a streak of jealousy over Fronie's cream pies, but she knew better than to ask for the recipe. Fronie guarded her cream pie recipes as closely as she would have guarded a mink coat if she had one—which she did not. She'd always secretly wanted one, but she publicly said that nobody except Davy Crockett ever wore fur in Tennessee. Everybody knew, of course, that Fronie's statement was sour grapes.

The table Ellen approached was practically buckling under the weight of food. Honey-glazed hams, fried chicken, pork and dumplings, competed for space with an assortment of delicacies that would have made a French chef green with envy. There was enough food to feed all the Stanfords, Ellen decided, and still have enough left over for half the population of Lawrence County. Except for Aunt Fronie's chocolate cream pie. She noticed that there was only one piece left, and Aunt Fronie was guarding it like Fort Knox.

She's still a handsome woman, Ellen thought as she came close enough to see the satin-smooth skin and the red hair, like her own, carefully twisted into a knot on top of Fronie's head. She knew Aunt Fronie took as much pride in preserving herself as she did in creating her famous pies. "Aunt Fronie"—Ellen kissed the old woman's cheek—"I've come for a piece of your pie."

Fronie pinched Ellen's cheek. "Lord, honey, you're even more beautiful than your mama was. And that man of yours . . ." She rolled her eyes and grinned. "Well, I said to Lollie, he ought to be in the movies. Rich, too, from what Vester tells me. When are you two tying the knot?"

"We haven't set the date yet." Ellen crossed her fingers behind her back as one more strand of untruth was added to the web of duplicity.

"A man like that, driving in the Grand Preakness and all . . . well, who knows what's on his mind," Fronie said. Ellen smiled. Her aunt never could get horse racing and automobile racing straight. "I wouldn't wait too long if I were you," Fronie went on. She took a funeral-parlor fan from her straw purse and swatted at the flies that were taking an interest in the picnic food. "About that pie, honey. I'm saving it for Dirk."

So he's made another conquest, Ellen thought. She supposed she should be happy that the deception was working so well, but suddenly it occurred to her that it wasn't supposed to work *that* well.

She had just wanted to get through this reunion without all the questions about when she was going to settle down and find a man. The way things were going now, her relatives would tar and feather her when she announced that she no longer intended to marry their hero. A gleam of mischief came into her eyes as she hastily devised a new plan.

She reached across Aunt Fronie's waving fan. "There's no need to save the pie for Dirk." She scooped it onto her plate and leaned over to whisper confidentially into her aunt's ear. "You know how I love doughnuts, Aunt Fronie?" Her aunt nodded solemnly. "Well, the last time we were out together, he ordered half a dozen and didn't give me a single bite. I could have died. He certainly didn't need them. You should have seen him before he lost all that weight." She tried to keep a straight face as she deliberately added clay feet to everybody's hero.

Aunt Fronie's fan skipped a beat as she digested the news, and Ellen decided that the plan was working beautifully. She didn't know why she hadn't thought of it sooner.

She felt her plate being lifted from her hand. "Don't you know all that sugar is bad for your digestion, darling?" Dirk said. He was standing behind her, grinning. He winked at Aunt Fronie. "She's mean as a copperhead snake when her digestion is upset."

As Aunt Fronie's mouth dropped open in disbelief, Dirk circled Ellen's waist with his free hand and leaned down to whisper in her ear. "How do you prefer your doughnuts? Plain or with icing?"

Ellen didn't bat an eyelash at being found out. She calmly took the pie out of his hand and tried to look crestfallen. "What did I tell you, Aunt Fronie? He's selfish, and a glutton to boot."

Aunt Fronie's generous mouth drew into a severe line. "I thought you said you had driven in the Grand Preakness."

Dirk controlled his laughter. "I did." He deftly took the pie back from Ellen. "Just looking after your health, my sweet pea."

Ellen snatched it back. "And I'm looking after yours."

Aunt Fronie watched her pie move back and forth between the people she had thought were perfect lovers. She was confused. She knew that only brave men drove racing cars in the Grand Preakness, and she did admire a brave man. She thought racing was even grander than fur coats, or even whales, for that matter. But she hated selfishness.

"I can't abide a stingy man," she announced as she took the pie from Ellen. "There's such a thing as sharing, you know." She bent over the table and picked up a knife.

Ellen put her hand on Aunt Fronie's. "Don't bother to divide that pie. I wouldn't give him a bite if he were on his knees begging." She emphasized her false anger by glaring up at Dirk. His shoulders were shaking with controlled mirth, and she dug her elbow into his ribs. She was beginning to enjoy this new role of outraged lover. She looked back at her aunt and tried another pout. She figured that by the time this reunion was over, she would have the pout down to an art. "Didn't you hear him call me a copperhead snake?"

"Did I do that?" Dirk hid his grin by leaning down to nibble her neck. "Let's kiss and make up, honey-bunchums."

As his lips touched her skin, shivers went down

Ellen's spine. She wasn't supposed to be enjoying her outraged lover role *that* much, she told herself. "Honey-bunchums?" she whispered in his ear as she twisted away. "Don't touch me, you cad," she said for Aunt Fronie's benefit. Leaning over the table, she scooped up the pie. "Go try your charms on that Waylings girl."

Aunt Fronie's mouth tightened even more. A lovers' quarrel was one thing, but another woman was something else altogether. If there was anything she hated more than a stingy man, it was a philandering man. "Who's the Waylings girl?" she asked.

"Ask Dirk," Ellen said.

By now quite a crowd had gathered at the scene of the fracas. Most of them were only mildly curious, and seeing that it was just a lovers' quarrel, they turned and walked away. Several of the Stanfords, however, loved nothing better than a good brawl. They wouldn't have missed the chocolate-pie incident—as it was later called—if they had been offered a free trip to Las Vegas, which was a mighty fine offer, for these same Stanfords also loved to gamble.

"Yeah, Dirk," a rawboned teenager with pimples said. "You'd better explain about the Waylings woman. We Stanfords don't cotton to anybody messing with the affections of one of our women."

Dirk's arm snaked back around Ellen's waist, and he pulled her close against his chest. "I would lay down my life for this woman," he assured the boy. "I never looked at another woman after I met her. Even burned my black book." He winked. "When she gets upset, she always drags in my former acquaintances. You know how that goes." Burying his lips in Ellen's hair he whispered, "Don't get carried away, darling."

Partly to continue the charade, but mostly to get away from his disturbing embrace, she waved the pie aloft and shouted, "I'll show you 'carried away.' "

Just at that moment Gigi, who had joined the group unnoticed, spotted the pie. She loved chocolate pie even more than she loved potato chips. With a grunt of delight she snatched the pie from Ellen's hand and gobbled it down in two bites.

This was the final straw for Aunt Fronie. A lovers' quarrel was fascinating, but her pie was sacred. Especially her chocolate cream pie. "Did you see that?" she shouted. "That *gorilla* ate my pie."

Gigi gave her a chocolate-covered grin and proceeded to lick the bits of meringue off her fingers.

"She loves pie, Aunt Fronie," Ellen said. "Especially your chocolate cream pie."

"But there was only one piece left."

"I know that," Ellen said, trying to sound soothing. She was relieved that Gigi had come along to take the attention away from the lovers' quarrel. She was afraid that she *had* carried it a bit too far. And now, if Dirk would just take his arm away, everything would return to normal.

"Don't worry, Aunt Fronie," he said. "Ellen and I will eat another dessert."

"But it won't be my pie," Fronie wailed.

Gigi finished cleaning the pie off her fingers and reached over to retrieve a fleck of chocolate that had spattered onto Aunt Fronie's arm. She popped the last morsel into her mouth, then turned a somersault to show her delight.

"Stop that, you big ape," Fronie yelled. "Eating my pie and then showing off."

"Aunt Fronie," Ellen cautioned, but it was too late.

Gigi didn't recognize the spoken words, but she knew the tone of voice. From her seat on the pavilion floor she signed up at Fronie.

"What did she say?" Aunt Fronie asked suspiciously.

The teenager with the pimples laughed. He had learned sign language when his cousin first started bringing Gigi to these reunions. He knew exactly what she had said. "She called you a dirty toilet seat, Auntie."

"Indeed! Well, I think you're a pig." It never occurred to Aunt Fronie, who prided herself on her dignity, that she was exchanging insults with a gorilla.

Her tone of voice again roused Gigi to action. She stuck out her tongue at Aunt Fronie, then defended her actions by signing to Ellen.

"Yes," Ellen signed back as she spoke aloud. "Gigi is a fine animal gorilla."

Everybody laughed except Aunt Fronie. "Humph," she said. "If you ask me, she's a spoiled brat."

"Aw, Aunt Fronie," the teenager said. "You're just mad because you lost the argument."

"Go wash behind your ears, Herbert," Fronie told him. "You always did have dirty ears." With that parting remark, Aunt Fronie held her head high and made a dignified exit.

Gigi spotted a coconut cream pie and quickly lost interest in everything except eating.

"Poor old love," Ellen said as she watched her aunt walk away. "I'm afraid we've ruined her day."

"She'll get over it," Herbert said as he and the rest of the crowd walked away.

"What about me?" Dirk asked. "I believe you've ruined my reputation."

Ellen laughed. "What reputation?"

He put his hands on her shoulders and slid them slowly down her bare arms. The sensuous abrasion made her catch her breath. "My reputation as a flag-waving citizen and a faithful lover."

"You can let me go now. The show is over."

He lifted one of her hands and planted a long, lingering kiss in her palm. "On the contrary, love. It's just begun." He pulled her roughly to him and tilted up her chin. "We have to kiss and make up, you know. Your relatives expect it."

Before she could protest, his lips descended onto hers, and she found herself being very thoroughly kissed. A fleeting thought crossed her mind that he didn't have to overdo it, and then she was lost in the magic of his embrace.

His lips were hot summer sunshine and mimosa and honeysuckle. The taste of him burned itself into her senses, and she knew that this was not pretend. This was a kind of magic that worked its way into the empty places of her heart and drove away the lonesomes. This was fire and tenderness, desire and sweetness. This was almost like coming home.

Lost, she thought. *I am lost.* Then he released her. She stood still for a moment, willing her drugged mind to work again. "You've undone everything," she said quietly. "You were supposed to stay tarnished so I could jilt you with impunity."

"That's okay, love." The unsettling gleam in his eyes belied the lightness of his voice. "We can have another fight."

"And make up again?" She didn't know why she said it. It just popped out.

He smiled. "If you like."

"Of course, I don't like," she said hotly. "I don't like anything about this charade. You're nothing but a bother." It was partially true, she told herself.

He was certainly a bother, but not in the way she had said.

"Did you know that your eyes look like green fire when you're upset?"

"Don't try to con me. I'm immune to your charms."

"Are you?" he asked. She thought his smile was wicked.

"Certainly."

"You don't know how charming I can be on a featherbed."

Her whole body went slack at the thought. "I don't intend to find out." Lifting her head in an exact imitation of Aunt Fronie, she marched stiffly away. The sound of his laughter floated after her, and she thought it was wicked too.

She spent the rest of the afternoon indulging in animated conversation with her aunts and cousins, and trying to forget about the maddening impostor who had swept through Lawrence County in the same manner that Sherman had swept through Atlanta. The only difference was that this time nobody had been burned except her.

It was over, Ellen thought. The long-awaited family reunion had come and gone, and now there was nothing left except to go back home and plunge into her work. She sat in the kitchen and listened to the drone of voices around her. Aunt Lollie was bringing her daughter Emmaline up to date on the latest happenings in Lawrence County, and Uncle Vester had Dirk and Emmaline's husband cornered, discussing his soybean crop.

Ellen felt as if the walls were closing in around her. Quietly she slipped from the room. She had to be alone. As she stepped onto the porch she heard the haunting call of a whippoorwill and the distant barking of a dog. She paused, lifting her face to the evening sky and drinking in the beauty of nature, then she sprinted toward the barn.

The heavy barn door creaked on its hinges, and White Fire whinnied in greeting. She patted the stallion's forehead. "Have you missed me?"

The white Arabian stallion tossed his head and snorted with excitement.

"Of course you have," Ellen said as she strapped the saddle onto his broad back. "There's nobody here anymore to ride you the way you should be ridden." She patted his flanks. "Someday I'm going to make a place for you and take you back to Beech Mountain."

She finished saddling the horse and sprang lightly onto his back. The worn leather bridle felt good in her hands as she guided White Fire through the barn door and out into the night. They galloped across the pasture at full speed with the moon and the stars lighting their way. Ellen felt a sense of exhilaration as the wind tossed her hair and the powerful hooves pounded the earth. The family reunion, Dirk, the deception—everything was forgotten except the wild freedom of the ride.

Together they thundered across the night-peaceful land until they came to a small creek on the back forty of Uncle Vester's farm. Ellen slid from the saddle and led White Fire down to the moonlit water for a drink. Then she looped the bridle around the branch of an oak tree and sat down in the crevice of one of its gnarled roots. Leaning her head against the tree trunk, she let her mind wander back over the events of the day, trying to sort her jumbled emotions and make sense of what had happened. Her thoughts circled restlessly, always coming back to Dirk. She tried to be remote and analytical, to approach Dirk as she would any other scientific problem, but it didn't work that way. There was nothing scientific about the way her pulse hammered and her knees went weak when he touched her. The rush of heat through her body couldn't be measured in a laboratory, and the remembered feel of his kisses refused to become footnotes in an experiment worksheet.

"Uncle Vester told me I would find you here." Dirk's voice shattered the stillness of the night.

She jerked her head around and saw him silhouetted against the evening sky. His powerful body was erect on Uncle Vester's old broken-down mule, Annie, but he seemed to be ill at ease with the bridle.

He was the last person in the world that she wanted to see, but she had to laugh at the way he looked on that mule. "You don't look like a man who rode in the Preakness," she said.

"I didn't. Horses and I don't speak the same language." He slid off Annie's back and tugged on the bridle.

Annie had been turned out to pasture fifteen years ago and she obviously had had all the nonsense she was going to take for one night. She dug her feet into the earth and refused to move.

Dirk cast a helpless look at Ellen. "How do I get her to move?"

"Like this." Ellen rose from her tree-root seat and took the bridle. Annie followed her like a lamb.

"How did you do that?"

"I speak her language."

"You certainly do. Stubborn."

"I won't be baited," she told him quietly.

He dropped to the ground and stretched out under the oak tree. "I'm not here to bait you, love."

"Why are you here?"

"That's what I hope to find out." He patted the ground beside him. "Join me, Ellen. It's lonesome down here."

She eased down beside him, being careful to put enough distance between them so that they weren't touching. She had already learned that touching this man was risky. Her fingers closed over a small twig and she picked it up. What was there about Dirk, she wondered, that always made her restless?

"Is Dirk really your name?" she asked.

"Yes."

"Caldwell?"

"No."

"What is your real name?"

He took the twig from her hand and snapped it in two. "My real name doesn't matter." He traced her jaw with the tips of his fingers. "Yours is a face that could launch a thousand ships," he said softly. She felt a tremor run through his fingers as they lingered on her face. "It's a face that could make a man forget."

She sat very still, hoping that the little flames he had set off inside her would go away. "What are you trying to forget? Tell me about yourself, Dirk."

He removed his hand. Ignoring the part about what he was trying to forget, he said, "I like dogs and cats and gorillas, but I don't get along with horses."

"How about cars?"

"The story I told Aunt Fronie?"

"Yes."

"It's true. I did drive in the Grand Prix. Once."

She let out a deep breath. So it was true. She thought back to the other things he had mentioned—Bengal tigers and Paris and being an orphan. How much of it was true? Who was he, this man who had come uninvited into the lonesome places of her heart? "Are you a man on the run?"

"You might say that."

"Are you dangerous?"

"Not to you." He reached across the small space that separated them and cupped her face with his hands. "Never to you."

They looked deep into each other's eyes, and the night seemed to embrace them with its velvet blackness. Ever so slowly she lowered her head until her lips were only a hairbreadth away from his. "I can't seem to fight it," she murmured.

"Nor can I." And knowing that he shouldn't, knowing that it would soon be impossible for him to turn and walk away, he embraced her, pulling her down beside him.

His lips brushed across her forehead, roamed down the side of her face, under her chin, and came to rest in the hollow of her throat. They lingered there, feeling the erratic beat of her pulse.

She arched against him, straining close, hungrily fitting herself to the hard lines of his body. Her hands were caught in the dark tangle of his hair as his lips moved down her throat and seared the cleft of her upthrust breasts. He nudged her shirt button open and his tongue traced the soft, curving outline of her breasts. The heat of a thousand ancient love-fires raced through her. She impatiently brushed aside the restraining bit of lace and freed her taut nipples. Dirk moaned low in his throat as he captured the dusky rose treasure in his mouth and began to suckle her. One of his legs moved across her hips and pulled her tight against his throbbing manhood.

She freed her mind of everything except the beauty of the night and the exquisite pleasure of the moment. Yesterday was a forgotten dream and tomorrow might never come. But for now, she had Dirk. Her body pressed against his as his tongue plied its magic. The sensuousness of his touch turned her loins to molten lava, and her mind soared up among the stars as he took her breast deep into his mouth.

She worked open the buttons of his shirt and slid her hands around to caress his back. She was still for an instant when she felt the ridges of the diagonal scar across his shoulder, then she succumbed to her drugged senses. Her fingers dug into his bare skin, marking it with her nails as his tongue and teeth pulled at her heavy, love-filled breasts. She felt his massive hardness straining against her clothes, and she moved against him in frantic rhythm.

Like a drunken sailor, he reeled up from her breasts and covered her mouth. His tongue plunged into her waiting warmth and engaged hers in a frenzied duel. Colored lights exploded inside her as she felt the moistness of her release. Her body went slack, and her tongue languorously explored his mouth.

She felt his hand move to the waistband of her jeans. "Yes," she murmured as he popped open the snap. The small sound seemed to explode in the tense night air. "Oh, yes." Her hands moved to find his belt buckle.

"No," he whispered harshly. Shaking his head like a man coming out of anesthesia, he raised up on his elbow and looked down at her.

"Dirk?" She reached up to caress his face, puzzled.

He covered her hand and held it there against his face. She was very still, watching him. She saw the pain flicker in his eyes, felt the clenching of his jaw.

"Why?" she asked.

He brought her hand around to his mouth and tenderly kissed her palm. "I've discovered a lot of things about myself since I've been your fiancé." He separated her fingers, pausing to kiss their tips, one by one, as he talked. "I've discovered that I have feelings. And scruples. And a code of honor, warped as it may be."

"I've known from the beginning that you are a man of honor." She sat up and pulled her blouse closed, waiting for him to continue.

"There are other things you don't know about me, Ellen. Things I can't tell you."

"Can't or won't?"

"Can't. I won't involve you in—" He stopped. He had almost said, "My work." His jaw tightened. Damn his work, he raged inwardly. Damn the danger and the need for secrecy. The very things that had drawn him to the CIA were now millstones around his neck. Fifteen years ago he had never dreamed that one day a woman would become this important to him.

He stood up abruptly. The only way to do this was quickly. There would be less pain that way. "I won't involve you in a summer affair, Ellen. You're too important to me." He watched her face as he talked. It remained calm and untroubled. If she felt any anger, any turmoil, it didn't show. Lord, she's incredible, he thought.

Ellen wanted to reach out and take him in her arms. She wanted to pull him down under the oak tree and make him forget scruples. She wanted to tell him that she was a big girl, that she could handle a summer affair. She wanted to scream.

She did none of those things. She gave him a

radiant smile. At least she hoped it was radiant. To her it felt slightly ragged around the edges. "Can you find your way back to the house?"

"Yes."

"I'll leave you, then." She untied White Fire, sprang into the saddle, and looked down at him. "With your warped code of honor." She dug her heels into the horse's flanks, and they were gone.

Dirk thought she looked magnificent in the moonlight, all fire and passion, like a beautiful avenging goddess. He watched the white stallion leap away, and strained his eyes until he could see nothing except the red halo of her hair and a distant speck of white. "Fool," he said, chiding himself. "All that could have been yours."

He walked to the bank of the creek and sat down. "It's just me and you, Annie," he said to his sagging mount.

The old mule lifted her head and brayed her condolences.

Ellen rode hard and fast. Her hair whipped about her head and the night wind stung her cheeks. The thundering rhythm of White Fire's hooves echoed in her head, but they could not drown out her tumultuous thoughts. A summer affair, he had said. That was what she wanted, wasn't it? A brief pleasure, a fling that would end when the leaves turned gold. A fleeting passion that wouldn't interfere with her work.

Who was she kidding? She wanted more. She wanted to know the man. Not just his body, but the whole man. His thoughts. His habits. What made him laugh. What made him cry. Her disjointed thoughts kept pace with the staccato hoofbeats in the sultry, summer night.

As the barn loomed into sight she decided that she should be grateful to Dirk. He had saved her from herself. She guided White Fire through the doors and unsaddled him. After rubbing him down and feeding him, she went back to the farmhouse. It was quiet except for the sounds of Aunt Lollie's snoring.

She ascended the staircase and dressed quickly for bed, trying not to think about the rest of the night. The soft featherbed beckoned to her, but she walked to the closet and took down the quilts. She had created this charade, she thought resolutely. From now on she would stick by the rules. It was her turn to sleep on the floor.

She lay down, expecting to toss and turn, but the long day took its toll. She was asleep almost as soon as her head touched the pillow.

Dirk had no idea what time it was. He had come so under the spell of this sleepy little Southern town where hours melted and ran together that he had not worn his watch today. He crept silently up the stairs, his years of experience in caution coming to his aid. Like a shadow he slipped through the bedroom door and stood still until his eyes had adjusted to the darkness.

Ellen was lying on her back on the floor, the covers kicked down to reveal her long, lovely legs. He shook his head, smiling. Stubborn, he thought, just like that old mule he had finally coaxed back to the barn. He should have known that she would be on the floor. After his dismissal of her beside the creek, he had known that she would become all business again, that this would be a charade, and he would be a hired fiancé. He felt as if a stone had been laid on his heart.

Bending down, he gathered Ellen into his arms and lifted her off the pallet. She sighed softly in her sleep and snuggled against his chest. He looked at her face and the stone in his heart became a boulder. "I should get a medal for this," he muttered as he walked across the room and gently deposited her on the bed.

Quickly, before he could change his mind, he took the car keys out of her purse. He knew that escape was the only answer for him tonight. Turning in the doorway, he gave her one last look. "Good night, my darling," he said, and then closed the door behind him.

Six

When Ellen woke up and saw that she was on the featherbed, she didn't know whether to laugh or cry. She glanced quickly around the room, but there was no sign of Dirk. She stumbled to the bathroom and splashed cold water on her face. She felt tired, as if she had been running all night and had come in dead last. It wouldn't do for Aunt Lollie to see her like this, she thought. Her aunt would prescribe the ham and egg cure.

Ellen took a leisurely bath and dressed with care. By the time she got downstairs, she looked as serene as sunshine on a summer day. "Good morning, Aunt Lollie." She kissed her aunt's plump cheek.

"Good morning, dear." Aunt Lollie turned from the chocolate pound cake she was making. If her forced cheerful tone hadn't alerted Ellen that something was amiss, the sight of her flour-spattered apron would have. Aunt Lollie never spilled a drop of flour when she cooked unless she was disturbed about something. "I kept your pancakes warm."

"Thanks, Aunt Lollie." Ellen went straight to the

old-fashioned stove. She had once offered to buy her aunt a microwave open, but Lollie had refused on the grounds that microwaves turned out rubber food and were dangerous to boot. The oven door felt warm to Ellen's touch, and there were enough pancakes inside to feed a camp of loggers. She forked two of them onto a plate and sat down at the kitchen table.

Aunt Lollie left the cake batter half mixed and joined her. Ellen put down the maple syrup she had been pouring over her pancakes and studied her aunt's face. When Aunt Lollie left her cooking, something serious was afoot. A cold fear gripped Ellen as she remembered how thin her uncle was. "Has something happened to Uncle Vester?"

"Vester?" Aunt Lollie laughed. "Don't you worry about your uncle." She patted Ellen's hand. "That darlin' old poop will still be around when I'm turning up daisies." She tried to draw her mouth into a severe line, but it didn't work. Aunt Lollie's mouth was made for laughter. "If he can stay out all night playing cards at Huck Henry's barn, he'll last long enough to dandle your babies upon his knee."

The pancake turned to sawdust in her mouth as Ellen thought of all the babies she wouldn't have. She washed the offending food down with milk. What did she need with babies? she scolded herself. She had Gigi. "That's a relief." She sought to turn the conversation away from her fantasy babies. "Will Emmaline and her family be joining me for breakfast? You have enough pancakes in the oven to feed an army."

"Those are for Dirk." The way Aunt Lollie said it, without preface and with a curious flatness, made Ellen glance up.

"He hasn't eaten yet?"

Aunt Lollie looked crestfallen. "Child, child," she consoled as she again patted Ellen's hand.

"Aunt Lollie, what's wrong?" Now Ellen was alarmed. Had something happened to Dirk? Last night she had left him with that ornery old mule. There was no telling where Annie had carried him.

"You don't know?"

"Know what, Aunt Lollie?"

"It's not my place to say anything." She avoided Ellen's eyes by rearranging the bib of her apron. "What goes on between two lovers is no business of mine. None a'tall." She looked back up at Ellen. "Eat your pancakes, dear. They're getting cold."

"I'm not going to eat a bite until you tell me what's going on."

"You've got that Stanford stubborn streak, just like your daddy." Aunt Lollie sighed heavily. "I guess a man has to sow a few wild oats before he settles down."

"Are you talking about Dirk or Uncle Vester?"

"They're all the same. Vester never could get it all out of his system, and when he told me about Dirk, playing pool for *money*—well, my heart just went out to you."

Ellen went limp with relief. Stifling her laughter, she ate her cold pancakes with renewed zest. "What has that scalawag been up to?"

"I think you have a right to know." Aunt Lollie took a deep breath and plunged into the sordid story. "Vester told me he was going to Huck Henry's barn last night after everybody went to bed. He always tells me. What can you expect from a man like that? He's still as lively as a grasshopper in the spring. He was wound up tight as a drum after the reunion dinner. Needed to get away. I understand, of course. Always have. It's just that sometimes these things can be so trying on a woman."

Ellen listened patiently while Aunt Lollie justified Uncle Vester's actions. Aunt Lollie always did that. Even though she considered Huck Henry's barn to be a hotbed of sin, she always found a reason to exempt her beloved Vester from any wrongdoing. For Aunt Lollie, Ellen knew that love was indeed blind. It was also very beautiful with those two.

"Well, of course," Aunt Lollie went on, "when your Dirk showed up, Vester was as surprised as he could be. Him not even wearing the yoke yet, as my sainted mama used to say, and here he is at Huck Henry's barn. Vester was so surprised he upped his bid a dollar and him holding nothing but a pair of fours."

"Who told Dirk about Huck Henry's games?"

"You'd best ask your uncle that. I never discussed a thing with Dirk except whales and babies."

Ellen hid her smile behind another bite of cold pancake. When it came time to inform the relatives that she wasn't marrying Dirk, perhaps she could soften the blow by telling them that she was taking up whale watching. "Tell me more about the games, Aunt Lollie. Who won?"

Aunt Lollie shook her head. "I do declare, Ellen. If you don't sound just like a Stanford! Gambling's in the blood, I reckon." She rearranged her apron once more. "Dirk did. Vester said he'd never seen anything as slick in all his life. First, that man of yours took the entire pot at pool and then he cleaned everybody out in the poker game. He must have won close to twenty dollars."

Knowing how serious Aunt Lollie was about this business at Huck Henry's barn, Ellen decided that she should play her part of the aggrieved fiancée to the hilt. "If he had to gamble, at least he didn't lose."

"I'm glad to see you taking it so well."

"I guess it's because I'm crazy about him and can't help myself, Aunt Lollie." She crossed her fingers behind her back.

"Love does overlook these little things. Not that I'm saying staying out all night and playing poker for money is a little thing, mind you. It can try the patience of a woman," Aunt Lollie said.

"It looks like I'm destined to be one of the martyred Stanford women, Aunt Lollie. But I plan to suffer in silence. Dirk's worth suffering for." She had to bite her tongue to keep from laughing.

"I'm delighted to hear you say that, love." Dirk's deep voice startled them both. The two women turned to see him lounging in the doorway. He looked as if he had just been dragged up from the pits of hell. Dark shadows circled his bloodshot eyes, and a night's growth of beard bristled on his cheeks.

"How long have you been standing there?" Ellen asked. He looked so weary, she felt almost guilty for having slept like a lamb.

"Long enough to know that you're crazy about me and can't help yourself." He crossed the room with maddening slowness and leaned over the back of her chair. "Is all forgiven, darling?"

With him standing so near, Ellen's bones turned to melted wax. Out of the corner of her eye she caught a glimpse of Aunt Lollie's beaming face. Play the game, she told herself. It's almost over. She lifted her hand to pat Dirk's cheek. "Of course . . ."

She never got to finish the rest of her sentence. Dirk captured her hand and lifted her out of the chair. Pulling her against his chest, he said hoarsely, "This is the best part. Kissing and making up."

Ellen thought he should win an Academy Award for the kiss. As his lips devoured hers, even she was almost convinced that it was real, that they were two people, crazy in love, making up after a dreadful misunderstanding. She tried to hold back, to play a convincing role without involving her feelings, but it was no use. His compelling power drained her will and sapped her strength. She found herself melting against him, responding to his demanding kiss with an abandon that would have shocked her if she had been sitting in Aunt Lollie's chair watching.

When the kitchen walls began to fade and the fireworks he had set off in her body threatened an explosion that would rock Lawrence County, Dirk pulled slowly away. "I'm beginning to get addicted to this," he whispered as his lips brushed her ear.

"You can ring down the curtain now, Dirk. The play is over." She spoke quietly so that Aunt Lollie wouldn't hear. She turned back to her aunt and noticed the look on her face. It was an expression of pure joy. Ellen decided that it made the deception worthwhile.

"Now, isn't that sweet," Aunt Lollie said. "Kissing beats ham and eggs for fixing things."

Ellen wasn't so sure about that. As much as she despised ham and eggs, she thought they would be considerably less dangerous than kissing.

Dirk chuckled. "I like the way you think, Aunt Lollie."

She rose from her chair and seemed to notice her apron for the first time. "Will you just look at me? I look like I've been dumped into the flour barrel. Will you children excuse me while I tidy up?" She patted Dirk's cheek. "As long as you love our Ellen, that's all that matters. Your breakfast is in the oven, dear. I'll be back as soon as I change my apron." With that she left the kitchen.

"That's a good-hearted, simple woman," Dirk said. "On the other hand"—he reached out and circled Ellen's waist—"you, my darling, are complex."

She couldn't bear his touch. It brought back vivid memories of last night beside the creek. It made her forget that their love was fantasy. She removed his hand as she turned the subject away from herself. "And you need a shave before we say good-bye to all the relatives."

"You disappoint me, love."

She knew she should let the remark pass, but she couldn't. "In what way?"

"Didn't you miss me last night?" The way he asked it, with a little-boy appeal in his voice, made her want to take him into her arms and smooth his tousled hair.

"No," she said. "I slept like a log."

"On the featherbed?"

"Yes."

"Aren't you curious about how you got there?"

"I don't want to know."

"I put you there. I picked you up and held you in my arms—"

"I don't want to hear any more."

"I looked at your beautiful body in the moonlight—"

"Please, Dirk."

"—and I wrestled with my conscience. You see, I've also discovered that I have a conscience."

"I'm sure you'll get over it," she said dryly. She didn't want to hear these things. Last night she had come too close to going off the deep end with him. She had come too close to forgetting what her life was all about. It was about language research

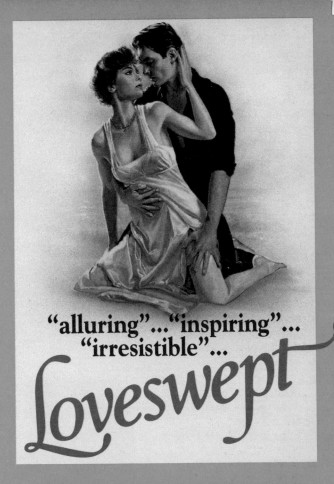

"alluring"... "inspiring"...
"irresistible"...

Loveswept

EXAMINE 4 LOVESWEPT NOVELS FOR

15 Days FREE!

Turn page for details

America's most popular, most compelling romance novels...

Loveswept

Here, at last...love stories that really involve you! Fresh, finely crafted novels with story lines so believable you'll feel you're actually living them!

Read a Loveswept novel and you'll experience all the very real feelings of two people as they discover and build an involved relationship: laughing, crying, learning and loving. Characters you can relate to... exciting places to visit...unexpected plot twists...all in all, exciting romances that satisfy your mind and delight your heart.

And now you can be sure you'll never, ever miss a single Loveswept title by enrolling in our special reader's home delivery service. A service that will bring all four new Loveswept romances published every month into your home—and deliver them to you *before* they appear in the bookstores!

Examine 4 Loveswept Novels for

15 Days FREE!

To introduce you to this fabulous service, you'll get four brand-new Loveswept releases not yet in the bookstores. These four exciting new titles are yours to examine for 15 days without obligation to buy. Keep them if you wish for just $9.95 plus postage and handling and any applicable sales tax.

with Gigi and a mountaintop compound. It was about long hours dedicated to science and sometimes a bone-weariness that sought nothing more than an empty bed. It was not about black-eyed men who hid an endearing vulnerability underneath a tough-guy facade. "Your breakfast is waiting," she said. "We leave in an hour." She whirled around and left the kitchen before she could change her mind. She was afraid of what she might say if she stayed.

Aunt Lollie and Uncle Vester were standing on the porch, arm in arm, as they watched Dirk and Ellen load the car.

"Don't drive like a hellion going home," Uncle Vester called to his niece.

"And don't forget to write," Aunt Lollie added.

Ellen turned to smile at them. "I won't."

"And bring that man of yours back real soon," Uncle Vester said. "I want him to teach me a few card tricks."

Aunt Lollie glanced coyly at her husband. "I want him to teach you how to kiss."

Uncle Vester roared with laughter. "Lordy mercy, woman. You'll be the death of me yet."

"Humph. I never knew a soul that died of too much lovin'," Aunt Lollie said.

Ellen and Dirk had returned to the porch in time to hear the exchange between the two old lovebirds. Dirk winked at Uncle Vester and hugged Aunt Lollie. "I never did either," he said. "Goodbye, Aunt Lollie."

She squeezed him to her ample bosom. "Just for a little while, son. We'll be at your wedding with bells on. You take care of our Ellen, now. You hear?"

Ellen thought that Dirk had a funny expression on his face when he released Aunt Lollie. He was probably glad that the charade was finally over, she thought. She supposed that he could hardly wait to get back to the mountains and forget the whole thing. She blushed at the way she had practically thrown herself into his arms last night. She would be happy to put this whole thing behind her too.

She kissed her aunt and uncle good-bye, promised to write, promised not to drive too fast—but kept her fingers crossed behind her back—and promised Aunt Lollie to try to cultivate a taste for eggs.

At last they were in the car, winding through the lane of oaks and kicking up dust as they headed home. Yes, indeed, she was happy it was all over, Ellen told herself. Then why did her heart feel lonesome? She kept her eyes on the road and tried not to think about that.

Dirk was strangely silent. She was afraid to look at him. She was afraid those black eyes would see right through her. She swore under her breath as a cow ambled across the road. Her tires squealed, as she skidded to the side of the road and stopped.

"You don't keep promises very well, do you?" Dirk said. His dark eyes were crinkled at the corners with amusement.

"Some promises weren't meant to be kept. Go back to sleep or whatever you were doing." She took a deep breath and pulled back onto the road.

"Do you want me to drive?"

"Are you afraid of my driving?"

"No. I've always thought a few concussions livened up a trip."

"So have I."

He chuckled. "That just goes to show you."

"To show what?"

"How much we have in common."

"We have nothing in common except a penchant for lying. I've told so many untruths at this reunion that my conscience will hurt for a month."

"But it was all for a good cause."

"That's what I keep telling myself." She made a left turn onto Uncle Mac's farm. After picking up Ruth Ann and Gigi and saying good-bye to Uncle Mac's family, the travelers began the long journey home.

For the most part it was a somber journey, the ending of an interval of make-believe. Only Gigi was in high spirits. Occasionally she cheered everyone up by insisting on singing a song that she had learned. It was a lively and rousing song with bawdy lyrics.

"Who taught her that?" Ellen asked, laughing, as Gigi sang with gorilla grunts and sign language.

"Those dreadful Wilcox twins," Ruth Ann said. Ellen thought that if her nose were pinched in any more she wouldn't be able to breathe.

"What's she saying?" Dirk asked.

"You don't want to know," Ruth Ann said.

"I'll tell you sometime if I ever get up the courage," Ellen told him.

By the time they reached Ellen's cabin, the setting sun had turned Beech Mountain into a rose-colored picture postcard. Ruth Ann went inside to prepare Gigi's evening meal while Dirk and Ellen unloaded the car. Gigi picked a bouquet of goldenrod beside the road.

Ellen deposited her bag on the porch and watched as Dirk loaded his gear in Rocinante. The charade was over, she thought. Time to get back to reality. She reached for her billfold as he returned to the porch to say good-bye.

"What are you doing?" he asked.

"I'm going to pay you."

"No."

"No?"

"I didn't do this because of the money. I went with you because I wanted to."

"But I hired you to do a job. You upheld your end of the deal, now I'm upholding mine." She pulled the money from her billfold and held it out to him.

His hand covered hers. "It was not just a deal with me. It was a pleasure." He removed his hand and shoved it into his jean's pocket. "Don't cheapen what we had with money."

"What did we have?" she asked softly. The money was trembling in her hand.

"For the short time that we allowed ourselves to feel, we had an interlude of romance. Thank you, Ellen." He turned abruptly and walked toward his car.

She watched him go. For a moment his shoulders sagged, then he lifted them and walked away in a show of jauntiness. She lifted her hand and almost called him back. The words were there, waiting to be said, but she couldn't make them come out.

As Ellen watched, Gigi shuffled up to Dirk and handed him the bouquet of goldenrod. She signed, *Man stay. Gigi love.*

Dirk lowered his head and sniffed the flowers. "These are nice," he said. "Thank you, Gigi." To Ellen's amazement he signed *Thank you.* She hadn't been aware that he was learning American Sign Language.

Gigi clapped her hands at Dirk's appreciation of her bouquet. *Stay. Man go. Gigi sad*, she signed.

Dirk solemnly took her hand. "Good-bye, Gigi. Thank you for the flowers."

Tears stung Ellen's eyes as Dirk climbed into Rocinante and headed toward Anthony's cabin. She watched until he was around the bend in the road.

Gigi lumbered up the porch steps and touched Ellen's cheek. *Ellen sad?* she signed.

"Yes, Gigi. Ellen sad," she said while signing.

Gigi sad too.

"Why?" Ellen signed. Dirk was temporarily forgotten as she did what she loved best, her work. To her the most amazing thing about her research was that Gigi expressed emotions. Although she knew why Gigi was sad, her question was aimed at encouraging the gorilla to think abstractly.

Man go. Gigi love. Gigi sad. The gorilla pointed to her own face. Her mouth was turned down in an exaggerated expression of sorrow.

"Happy good," Ellen said as she signed. "Sad good too. Make Gigi fine animal gorilla."

Gigi fine animal gorilla? Gigi's expression of sorrow was immediately replaced with a toothy grin. She loved compliments.

"Yes," Ellen assured her.

Gigi clapped her hands. *Fine animal gorilla hungry. Eat pie.*

Ellen grinned at the devilish expression on Gigi's face. The gorilla knew that pie was for special occasions. She was playing on Ellen's sympathy. "No," Ellen signed. "Gigi eat fruit. Eat vegetables. Good food."

No. Food stink. Gigi eat pie.

"Maybe," she said. "After vegetables." Ellen took her hand and led her into the house.

As Ellen watched Gigi finish her meal—she had relented about the pie—she wished that she could put Dirk from her mind as easily as Gigi. She wished pie would make her forget. She thought about the parting and decided that Gigi had handled it with more thoughtfulness and compassion than she had. Gigi had given Dirk flowers and she had given him money. Almost, she corrected herself. She had almost ruined a relationship with thirty pieces of silver. She wondered if civilization got in the way of relationships. Was it possible that civilized trappings stifled love and romance and caring? Was it possible that love could not grow unless people forgot rules and codes of behavior and returned to primitive emotions?

She was still pondering these things when Ruth Ann led Gigi off to prepare her for bed.

Ellen went to her office to bring her notes up-to-date. Her mind kept wandering back to Dirk, and she finally threw her pen down in disgust. The ringing of the telephone was a welcome interruption.

"Hi. It's me," Rachelle said. Ellen smiled. Rachelle always identified herself that way. "How was the trip?"

"Fine."

"Fine? Fine! You return from a romantic weekend with a Tom Selleck look-alike and all you can say is fine?"

"Who told you?"

"You did," Rachelle said. "Before you left. While you could still drool and palpitate. Tell me everything."

"Aunt Lollie and Uncle Vester are still two wonderful lovebirds. They're as timeless as Beech Mountain. Glenda is still the family failure for having married beneath herself. Aunt Fronie still makes a great chocolate cream pie. . . ."

"What about Dirk? What did your family think of him?"

"He passed muster with flying colors."

"What did you think of him?"

The question caught Ellen off-guard. She shouldn't have been surprised, she reminded herself. Rachelle had been monitoring her love life—or lack of one—for the last five years. "It doesn't matter what I think of him. Besides, I don't even know what he does for a living."

"Good grief. You're off with a movie star and all you can think about is his job? Check out the body first, and then worry about the job." Rachelle giggled. "If you ever get around to it."

"That's one of the things I love about you, Rachelle. You don't let mundane things like jobs worry you. You live in a fantasy world."

"Yeah. It's filled with fabulous faces and great bods."

Ruth Ann appeared at the doorway. "Gigi won't go to bed," she said.

Ellen covered the mouthpiece. "I'll be right with you," she told her assistant. To Rachelle she said, "Duty calls. Can you leave your shop long enough to come up tomorrow for lunch? We can talk."

"Can do. See you tomorrow."

Ellen replaced the phone and walked through the compound to take care of Gigi's problem.

"What would we do without frozen croissants?" Ellen said. She pushed her plate away and reached for her glass of iced tea. A breeze stirred the branches of a pine tree overhead, and a couple of cardinals hopped close to the picnic table, hoping to catch a fallen crumb.

Rachelle took a bite of her croissant and leaned across the redwood table. "I didn't come all the way up Beech Mountain to get a Julia Child lecture.

Tell me about Dirk. I want to know everything that happened in Lawrenceburg."

"Nothing happened."

"Why do I get the feeling that you're holding back?" Rachelle studied her friend's face. "If I didn't know you better, I'd say that you were smitten."

"Smitten?"

"Don't play dumb with me, Doctor. Smitten as in head-over-heels, crazy, mooney-eyed. *In love*, for gosh sakes!"

Ellen marveled at how close her friend was to the truth. "If you're talking about Dirk . . ."

"Did I hear someone call my name?" Dirk walked out of the forest and into the clearing.

Ellen thought she would die on the spot. She had forgotten how impossibly handsome he was and how her heart wouldn't behave when he was around and how her bones turned to maple syrup. Why did he have to lean against the table with those fabulous hips? Why couldn't he stand over there on the edge of the woods so she wouldn't notice his chest gleaming through that half-buttoned shirt?

"Aren't you going to introduce me?" Rachelle's voice brought her back to reality.

"Rachelle Durante. Dirk—" Ellen hesitated, not knowing what to call him.

"Just call me Dirk," he said smoothly. He gave Rachelle a dazzling smile. "You must be the one who arranged for Nate."

Rachelle tossed her blond head and laughed. "I'll have to admit that Ellen did better on her own. Maybe you can tell me about the reunion. I can't get a thing out of the good doctor."

"Uncle Vester and Aunt Lollie are two of the finest people I've ever met," he said.

Rachelle rolled her eyes. "Here we go again."

"She doesn't want a report," Ellen explained. "She wants fantasy." For the first time she noticed the bouquet of wild flowers in his hand. "Why are you here?"

"I was out walking and saw these flowers. They reminded me of Gigi, so I decided to come by and see her. Is that possible?"

Ellen didn't know what she had expected him to say or why she felt a twinge of disappointment. "I'm glad you came back. For Gigi's sake," she added hastily. "It's good for her to know that friends can come and go."

"Then I'll go up to the compound," he said. "Don't bother to get up. Ruth Ann can let me in." He inclined his head toward Rachelle and smiled again. "It was nice meeting you, Rachelle."

Ellen forced herself not to turn around and watch him walk toward the compound. She forced herself to drink her tea as if her heart weren't doing a tap dance against her rib cage.

"Well, what do you know about that!" Rachelle said as soon as Dirk was out of earshot.

"About what?"

"Where is he staying? I didn't think there was anything up here except this compound and Anthony's cabin."

"That's where he's staying. Anthony's cabin."

"Well, what do you know about that!" Rachelle said again.

"Why do you keep saying that? For goodness' sakes, drink your tea and get that expression off your face."

Rachelle playfully pretended to wipe the expression off her face. "There. Is that better? Don't tell me that man was out walking and just happened to come three miles out of his way to deliver flowers. To Gigi yet!"

"There's nothing unusual about that. He happens to like Gigi. He has a great capacity for caring." If anyone had told Ellen how her eyes sparkled when she defended Dirk, she wouldn't have believed them.

"I'm sure he does," Rachelle agreed. "And from the way he fit into those jeans, I'd say he has a great capacity for something else too. Lucky you." She sighed lustily.

Ellen didn't even hear her. She was too busy thinking about that endearing little-boy look on Dirk's face and the wilted bouquet of wild flowers in his hand.

Seven

After Rachelle had gone, Ellen hurried back to the compound. As she passed the pine tree that marked the edge of the fenced-in area, she told herself that her haste was due to the work that needed to be done. A persistent picture of Dirk and his bouquet kept flitting through her mind, and by the time she reached the patch of goldenrod, she knew that she had been lying to herself. Dirk was the reason for her hurry.

Ruth Ann looked up as Ellen burst through the front door. "I see that you already know he's here," she said.

"How did you know?"

"You look like you've been in a footrace."

Ellen hastily repinned her loose topknot and put her hands to her flushed cheeks. Was she that transparent? "I have to reorganize my notes."

She started to walk briskly to her desk, then changed her mind. What was the matter with her? she wondered. She didn't need excuses for her actions. Who did she think she was fooling anyhow? Certainly not Ruth Ann. She stopped in midstride. "Where is he?"

"I thought you'd never ask." The starchy old scientist almost smiled. "He's in the dayroom with Gigi, drawing pictures."

Ellen whirled through the door and hastened down the hall. She stopped outside the dayroom door to smooth her white lab jacket and catch her breath. It would never do for Dirk to see her eagerness. As skittish as he was about things such as involvement and commitment, he would probably run all the way back to Paris or Connecticut or wherever he had come from.

She stepped into the room and stood quietly, observing the two artists. Drooping wild flowers were tucked behind Gigi's ears, and her head was cocked to one side as she studied Dirk's painting.

"What do you think, Gigi?" Dirk asked.

Gigi put her tongue between her lips and made a sound of disgust. "Bleah!"

"Is that an unbiased opinion, or do you have something against still lifes?" he asked.

"Bleah!" Gigi said.

"She fancies herself quite an art critic," Ellen said. She walked toward them, smiling. "You should hear what she says about my paintings."

Ellen wondered if she dreamed the amber light that leaped into his black eyes. Feigning nonchalance, she lifted Gigi's painting from the easel. The abstract drawing, done in red, faintly resembled a heart.

"Good, Gigi," she said while signing. "Tell Ellen picture name."

Love, signed Gigi.

Ellen taped the painting onto the wall and put a clean sheet of paper on the easel. "Gigi paint again." She turned to Dirk as Gigi carefully selected a yellow paint pen from the box. "I'm always amazed when Gigi paints," she told Dirk.

What she wanted to say was *I've missed you.* She pointed to a picture done in black. "She calls this one *Hate.*" What she wanted to say was *Hold me.*

Dirk walked over to her so that he could examine Gigi's artwork. Ellen drew a shaky breath as his shoulder touched hers.

"Incredible," he said. But he wasn't talking about the paintings. He was marveling once again at the way Dr. Ellen Stanford could make him feel vulnerable.

"This one," Ellen said, pointing to a black and white painting, "is a picture of her pet cat." She wondered if she could make the tour last forever.

Dirk moved closer to her, ostensibly to get a better view of the painting. "I didn't know she had a cat." What he wanted to say was *I can never forget the fragrance of your hair.*

"She calls him Spot." The minute she turned to look at him, Ellen knew she'd made a mistake. There he was: the fake fiancé who had somehow managed to become real, the artful deceiver who had worked his way into her heart. "Dirk." The softly spoken word was almost a plea as she put her hand on his arm.

His carefully built barriers began to topple as he gazed into her face. "Ellen." It was almost a sigh. He lowered his head, irresistibly drawn to her lips.

Like the touch of a butterfly, his lips brushed hers. Sweet, so sweet, he thought as he wrapped her in his arms, pulling her close enough to feel the hammering of her heart. Her lips parted beneath his, and for a few precious moments he drank the forbidden nectar. The light fragrance of her hair, the feel of her body next to his, the taste and texture of her mouth—all settled into his heart and became a part of him.

And then, one by one, he put the barriers back in place. Before the passion of her lips could drug him into a false sense of security, before the urgent message of her body could make him believe that love was for him, he ended the kiss.

"Ellen!" His voice was broken, and he held her fiercely to him before letting her go. Forbidden, his mind warned him. Love is danger; love is vulnerability; love is risk. At last he dropped his arms. "Good-bye, Dr. Ellen Stanford."

"Stay," she said as he turned to walk away.

"I can't." He smiled sadly at her over his shoulder. "I should never have come back."

"But you did."

"Yes. I did."

"Not just to see Gigi."

"No. I lied about that."

"There seems to be a lot of lies between us."

"Too many, Ellen." Turning away, he put his hand on the doorknob and stood there, hesitating, hoping that she would call to him again. But there was no sound from the room except the scratching of Gigi's paint pens. He walked through the door and closed it soundlessly behind him. "Don't look back," he said to himself as he walked down the empty hallway and into the real world.

Ellen looked at the closed door. "I won't cry!" she said aloud. Squaring her shoulders she walked to the easel to examine Gigi's painting. "He keeps doing me favors," she muttered. "I should be writing him thank-you notes." She wondered wryly if she were going to become one of those absentminded scientists who mumbled to herself all the time.

Telling herself that she was well rid of Dirk, she concentrated on recording Gigi's day. But from time to time she reached up and touched her lips.

* * *

The minute Ellen woke up, she knew that something was wrong. She lay in bed, listening. The compound was quiet—too quiet. She slipped into her robe and grabbed a flashlight from her bedside table. Tiptoeing down the hall, she peeked into Ruth Ann's bedroom. The door was slightly ajar, and she could see her assistant curled into a tight ball in the middle of her bed, snoring peacefully.

Ellen hurried through the double doors that led to Gigi's sleeping quarters. In the summertime the gorilla preferred sleeping outside. She peered frantically ahead, trying to make out Gigi's sleeping form in the predawn gloom. As her eyes adjusted to the dim light they confirmed what she instinctively knew: Gigi was not there.

"Gigi," Ellen called, knowing that there would be no answer. She went through the gate and turned her flashlight beam on the gorilla's pallet. Her covers had not been moved. They were neatly folded inside the gazebo that served as Gigi's nest.

Ellen knelt on the planked floor and examined the covers. Gigi's favorite quilt, the one with the gingham dog and the calico cat, was missing. Forcing herself not to panic, she walked around the edge of the fence, looking for possible means of escape. It didn't take long to find. One section of the heavy chain-link fence sagged dramatically where the two-hundred-pound gorilla had climbed over.

Ellen's feet practically flew over the ground as she ran back into the main building. "Ruth Ann," she shouted, "wake up. Gigi's gone." She had already stripped off her nightgown and stepped into her shorts when her assistant rushed into the room.

"How did she get out?" Ruth Ann asked. Although she looked like a sleepy, disheveled owl without her glasses, she was fully awake.

"She climbed over the fence," Ellen said as she hastily pulled on a thin cotton blouse.

"She's never done that before."

"I know." Ellen grabbed a flight bag off the top shelf of her closet and threw a first-aid kit inside. "She's close to the mating age. She's probably just prowling in the woods." Suddenly she stood very still. "Oh, no," she said almost to herself.

"What is it?" Ruth Ann asked.

"I think I know where she is."

"I'm not sure I want to hear this."

"You remember how dejected she was after Dirk brought the bouquet and left without telling her good-bye?"

Ruth Ann made new lines in her already severe face as she tightened her mouth. "Yes."

"And you know how she adores riding. Well, I took her for a ride. When we passed Tony's cabin, I pointed it out to her and told her that Dirk was staying there." She shook her head in self-disgust and jerked the zipper of her bag shut. "I never dreamed she would do this."

"Maybe she's just playing games with us. You know how she loves games."

"You don't believe that any more than I do." Ellen glanced out the window. "It's almost dawn now. As soon as it's light enough, make a circuit around the edge of the compound." She tried to sound optimistic as she spoke to her assistant. "Just in case she *is* playing games."

"Right." Ruth Ann pretended to believe in that possibility. "You're going to Anthony Salinger's cabin." It was a statement more than a question. "Pity he doesn't have a telephone."

"Yes. I'm going to walk in case Gigi doesn't have much of a head start. As soon as you've checked the perimeter of the compound, come inside and wait. It's too soon to panic. And we won't call reinforcements unless it's absolutely necessary. We don't want to spook Gigi."

"I knew he was trouble the minute I laid eyes on him."

Ellen ignored that remark. "I'm going to the kitchen to get some food. Wait until it's light, Ruth Ann, and be careful. If Gigi's there, I'll get Dirk to bring us back in his car."

"Be careful yourself. And I'm not just talking about the woods."

Ellen ignored that remark too. Taking her flashlight and her flight bag, she headed for the kitchen. She quickly chucked some bananas and granola bars into the bag and stepped outside. The first pale columns of light were filtering through the dense forest, and the branches of the trees were still heavy with dew.

Ellen entered the forest without fear. Beech Mountain had been her home for so long. She was familiar with every tree and rock within a five-mile radius of the compound. If Gigi hadn't been missing, she would have enjoyed her exploration of the woods. She thought the hour of dawn was the most tranquil of all. Nature's daytime creatures were stirring, celebrating the new day with jubilant calls, and her nighttime creatures were scurrying through the forest, seeking their various holes and burrows of rest.

Ellen used her flashlight in the dense forest, turning the beam on probable hiding places and calling Gigi's name. She scared up a rabbit and a family of wrens, but there was no sign of the gorilla. The forest floor was cushioned with compost—fallen trees and leaves from other seasons—so that, even if she had been an experienced tracker, finding signs of the gorilla's route would have been difficult.

Ellen estimated that she was at least a mile from the compound when she sat down on a fallen tree trunk to eat a granola bar. She could see shafts of gold through the treetops, but the branches were too thick to allow the sunshine to touch the forest floor. She hurriedly ate her makeshift breakfast and then resumed her search, leaving the crumbs for a pair of bluejays.

The trees began to thin as she came closer to Anthony Salinger's cabin. A bramble snagged her shirt, and as she stopped to loose herself she noticed a pink thread caught in the bush. Gigi's quilt, she thought. She walked faster, certain now that she knew where to find her runaway gorilla.

The dew was still on the grass when Ellen burst into the clearing beside Anthony's summer place. "Gigi," she called. A large, dark bundle on the front porch stirred.

Laughing and crying at the same time, Ellen ran toward the cabin. "Gigi," she called again. This time the bundle rose to its feet.

With her quilt tucked under her arm and dragging in the dirt behind her, Gigi loped toward Ellen. *Gigi happy see Ellen*, the gorilla signed.

The cabin door flew open. "What's going on?" Dirk stood on the porch in a pair of cutoff jeans.

Seeing him like that, bright-eyed and tousle-haired from recent sleep, Ellen forgave his disruption of her life. She forgave his sudden appearances and abrupt disappearances. She forgave the kisses that ended too soon. She forgave the passion that was offered and then withdrawn. She even forgave his role in Gigi's escape.

"Gigi ran away," she said. Taking the gorilla by the hand, she led her back to the porch.

"To see me?" Dirk asked.

"Yes." Ellen didn't elaborate.

"I'm sorry, Ellen." He reached out to touch her face, but Gigi intervened.

Grabbing Dirk's hand, she lifted it to her face, then dropped it to sign *Gigi find man. Gigi happy.*

Ellen almost envied her gorilla. She felt joy in Dirk's presence, too, but she couldn't express it. There were too many barriers between them, too many secrets.

He patted Gigi's head. "I like you, too, Gigi," he said. Turning to Ellen, he added, "If I had known she was out here, I would have brought her back." He looked down at Ellen's wet shoes. "You walked through the woods?"

"I didn't know when she had escaped. I thought I might find her closer to the compound."

"Come inside. I'll make coffee and eggs while you dry your feet." He held the door open.

"Ruth Ann's waiting. We really should get back."

But Gigi had other ideas. Grabbing Dirk's and Ellen's hands, she pulled them through the door. *Gigi hungry,* she signed to Ellen. *Long time food none.*

"It looks like I've been outvoted," Ellen said. She unzipped her bag and took out the fruit. "Gigi eat, then go home," she instructed her gorilla.

Gigi shook her head vehemently. *No. Gigi stay man's home. Gigi love man.*

"Problems?" Dirk asked. Even if he hadn't known the sign for *no*, he knew the meaning of that stubborn headshake.

"It looks like I'm dealing with a lovesick gorilla," Ellen said. "It's a pity you couldn't be a handsome ten-year-old four-hundred-pound male gorilla."

He laughed. "I qualify on only one count. I'm male."

Two counts, she thought. He was also handsome. As he turned to the stove to start the coffeepot, she saw the jagged six-inch scar on his back. No matter how many times she saw that scar, she was always shaken by what it symbolized—danger, brute force, secrets. She wished for the power to wipe his back clean of that telltale evidence. If there were no scar, perhaps there would be no barriers.

"Ellen." She became aware that Dirk was talking to her. "I've asked you twice if you want eggs."

"No. I don't want eggs. I want to know who you are."

"The scar?"

"Yes."

"It's an old wound and an old story, Ellen."

"Tell me."

"No. It's best forgotten." He poured the coffee into two cups and brought them to the table. "Sugar?"

"I don't want sugar; I want the truth."

"No, Ellen. I won't involve you." How could he tell her that the scar was his badge of honor? he wondered. How could he tell her that it represented triumph as well as danger? Danger: He felt a burst of adrenaline at the mere thought of the word. Danger coupled with challenge, the twin sirens that brought him back to his work time and again. He was silent for a moment as he gazed out the window at the serenity of Beech Mountain. What a contrast to the things he was used to seeing, he mused. "It seems impossible that bad things exist in such a beautiful world," he said, almost to himself.

Ellen watched his eyes as he talked. He seemed to be gazing into a crystal ball that held the history of the past as well as the mysteries of the future. Although he was sitting beside her at the table, he had gone to a place where she couldn't be, a lonely place with room for only one.

He picked up his cup and looked at her over the rim. "I care too much for you to let anything happen," he said.

"I'm a grown woman, Dirk. I don't need looking after."

"It's more than that." He reached out and covered her hand. "I wish I could—" Abruptly he released her hand. "Your coffee's getting cold."

Ellen stood up. "It's not the only thing getting cold," she said. She put a polite smile on her face and forced herself to remain on her side of the barrier. She had wasted enough emotions for one day. "Gigi's finished. Will you take us back to the compound?"

"Certainly."

The chill between them seeped into Ellen's bones and made her shiver. Dirk, too, seemed to be feeling its effects. His jaw was clenched so tight that the tiny scar was white.

Gigi was the only one who didn't suffer from the chill. She clapped her hands and turned somersaults when she found out that Dirk would be going back with them. Wrapping her quilt around her head, turban-style, she announced to Ellen, *Gigi wear nice blanket hat.*

The laughter broke the tension. Dirk gallantly held open the front door. "Come along, ladies. Rocinante awaits."

Gigi balked when she saw Rocinante. *Toy car?* she signed to Ellen.

"No, Gigi. Small car. Not toy," Ellen said, signing.

Gigi shook her head. *Toy car. Gigi not ride toy car.*

"What's she saying?" Dirk asked.

"She's never ridden in anything except my over-size Buick," Ellen explained. "She thinks this Mercedes is a toy car."

"Perhaps if I get in first, she'll follow," he suggested.

"Good idea." Ellen turned to her reluctant gorilla. "Man ride small car." She pointed to her-self. "Ellen ride small car. Gigi ride too."

No. Gigi sat on the ground and began to pick the grass.

Ellen sat beside her. "Please, Gigi," she signed. "Big car good. Small car good too."

Small car fly? Gigi asked.

"No."

"Bleah!" Gigi stuck out her tongue.

Dirk got out of the car. "Perhaps I can persuade her."

"It's worth a try. I'll interpret."

He sat beside them on the side of the road. Ellen thought wryly that if anyone happened along to see the two of them earnestly talking to the turbaned gorilla, he would probably notify somebody with a net.

"Tell her that the car is mine," Dirk said. "Tell her I'm sad that she won't ride in my car."

Ellen looked at the mirth sparkling in his eyes. "If you want her to fall for that, you'd better look lugubrious."

He dropped his mouth at the corners. "How's that? Is that mournful enough?"

Ellen didn't have time to reply. Gigi touched Dirk's face. *Man sad?*

"Man sad," Ellen confirmed. "His car." She pointed to Rocinante. "Good car. Man sad Gigi not ride his car."

Gigi unwrapped the quilt from her head and solemnly draped it over Dirk's shoulders. Pointing to the gingham dog and the calico cat, she signed, *Nice animals. Comfort man.*

Dirk held his laughter in check as he looked at Ellen. "Is this good?"

"I'm not sure. At least she's not shaking her head now."

Gigi touched Dirk, then stood up. *Good car,* she signed.

"Yes, Gigi, it is a good car," Ellen signed back. "I think she's coming around," she told Dirk.

Gigi gave them both a brilliant gorilla smile and signed grandly to Ellen.

Ellen burst out laughing.

"Did we succeed?" Dirk asked.

"Too well, I'm afraid. She told me, 'Gigi drive. Make car fly.'"

He chuckled. "What do we do now?"

"I don't know. This was your idea."

"Yes. But she's your gorilla."

Ellen studied her pupil. "Well, why not?" she finally said.

"You're not suggesting what I think?"

"Look at her. She's intelligent. She's coordinated." She smiled at Dirk. "Haven't you ever taught a sweet little old lady to drive?"

"Yes. But she didn't weigh two hundred pounds, and she couldn't bend steel bars with her bare hands."

"Do you have a better idea?"

"We could walk."

"We could," Ellen agreed. She explained to Gigi that they would walk back to the compound.

Gigi sat on the ground again and stuck out her tongue. *Poor Gigi. Feet hurt.* She pointed to her feet and to her sad face. *Poor Gigi. Tired animal gorilla. Not walk.*

Dirk looked down at Gigi. "I take it she said no."

"Right."

"Hell. I've always wanted to teach a gorilla how to drive."

While Gigi was sitting on the ground pouting, Dirk and Ellen devised a plan so that she would sit between them on the front seat and be allowed to do a few simple things that would make her believe she was driving. The dew was gone from the ground when the trio finally assembled in the toy car and started down the mountain.

With Dirk behind the wheel and Ellen instructing, Gigi turned the key in the ignition. She grunted with delight when the aging Mercedes sputtered to life. Next she investigated the radio button. Her hands moved rapidly across the dashboard as she "drove" down the mountain.

To Ellen and Dirk the three miles seemed like thirty. They arrived at the compound with the headlights glaring, the windshield wipers going, the cigarette lighter plugged in, the heater melting their feet, and Hank Williams bursting their eardrums with "Your Cheatin' Heart."

"Hallelujah!" Ellen said.

"Amen," Dirk said.

Smart animal gorilla, Gigi signed.

Ruth Ann hurried out to greet them. Ellen told her the story of their trip, then briefed her about Gigi's day. "I have to go into Banner Elk and consult an expert about the fence. We have to make it escape-proof."

"Why seek an expert in Banner Elk when you have one right here?" Dirk asked after Ruth Ann and Gigi had gone inside.

"You know about fences?"

"Yes."

She didn't doubt him. It was just one more tiny

piece of the puzzle, one more scrap of information to help her solve the mystery of the man.

She looked at his bare chest, bronzed by the sun, at the small scar on his jaw, at his amber-lit black eyes. A sensible voice of caution inside her said to send him home. It told her that having him around after all that had happened between them would be dangerous. The analytical, scientific side of her was yelling "Help!" as the romantic side of her longed to hide in the shelter of his arms.

"Stay and help me," she said simply. She wondered if she was asking for help with the fence or for help with her heart.

Two hours later Dirk and Ellen stood beside the heavier chain-link fencing and steel crossbeams that had been sent up from Banner Elk.

"I assume Gigi has another place to sleep while the fence is being replaced," Dirk said.

"Yes. She'll come inside to her winter quarters." Ellen looked at the heavy mass of fencing. "How long will this job take?"

"Two days if I do it alone. We can be finished by late this afternoon if you want to find somebody to help me."

"There's no need for you to stay now, Dirk. I'll get somebody else to put up the fence." Even as she said it, she knew that finding a crew to do a job like this might take days.

"No, Ellen. I want to stay."

Her heart flipped over, but the tiny voice of reason told her not to make too much of his statement. "Then I'll help you."

He laughed. "Are you handy with a hammer and a post-hole digger?"

"I can do anything that I make up my mind to do.

With me as your assistant, we probably won't finish today; but that's okay. Being confined to her winter quarters on a beautiful summer night will be a good punishment for Gigi."

A camaraderie developed between them as they worked side by side in the glaring sun. Dirk's admiration for Ellen grew as she tackled the heavy work with the same intensity that he had seen her apply to her research. Sweat trickled down the side of her face, and damp tendrils of hair clung to her forehead.

"Where were you when I was in Milan?" he asked.

"Cutting my teeth on a claw hammer," she teased. "What were you doing in Milan?"

"Helping an order of Dominican nuns build a fence."

"You were in a convent!"

"Yes. Posing as a nun."

"Apart from other obvious differences, didn't your beard shadow give you away?"

"The sisters were hiding me. They made up a tragic story about how I had been disfigured by falling face-first into a stewpot. They called me Sister Grendel."

"Who were you hiding from?"

"The best I can remember, it was an irate girlfriend." Up until that point he had been telling the truth. He decided that there was no need to spoil the day by mentioning organized crime. "Hey," he said lightly. "Are you going to hog the nails?"

"Hog the nails? Now where did a dyed-in-the-wool Connecticut whale watcher pick up an expression like that?"

"From your Uncle Vester. Remember Huck Henry's infamous card game?"

"How could I forget?"

"Uncle Vester accused Huck of hogging all the aces."

"If I know Huck, he probably was."

"Right. He had two of them up his sleeve."

Ellen wiped her face with the back of her arm. "Do we ever take a break from this fence building, or do you intend for me to expire on the spot?"

"I thought you were the boss."

"Well, why didn't you say so before?" She threw down her hammer and cocked her head to one side. "I'll race you to the refrigerator." She was ahead of him like a flash. "Last one up the hill is a rotten egg," she called.

He watched her run, enjoying the sight of her trim hips and limber legs in motion. And then he put down his tools. He sprinted past her with long, loping strides and was leaning casually against a cedar post on the porch when she arrived, flushed and panting.

"Lady," he said, affecting a Southern drawl, "if you aim to keep up with me, you'd better get in shape."

Tossing her head and propping her hands on her hips, she spoke indignantly. "Desist with the insults, sir, or I'll have my pappy horsewhip you." She was grinning as she joined his game.

"Can it wait until after the lemonade?"

She pretended to be in deep thought. "I fancy it can," she finally told him.

He laughed. "Fancy indeed." Grabbing her hand, he pulled her through the door. "Come on, rotten egg, before I die of thirst."

The bantering continued as they poured tall glasses of the ice-cold lemonade and wiped their sweaty faces on a dish towel.

"What's this?" Dirk asked. The dish towel was

stenciled with the words HAVE YOU KISSED THE COOK TODAY? "Where's the cook?" He pretended to search the kitchen, then suddenly pulled Ellen into his arms. "Ah, there's the cook." He brushed his lips, still cold from the lemonade, against her forehead. "Nice cook," he said, imitating Gigi. "Pretty damn good carpenter too. Make hammer fly."

If he hadn't said those ridiculous things, she probably would have swooned against his sun-warmed bare chest and died of happiness. She considered it a stroke of luck that he released her when he did. Otherwise she might have pulled him down to the kitchen floor and devoured him. She decided that animal magnetism or physical attraction or whatever it was had made Dr. Ellen Stanford take leave of her senses.

Dirk took her hand and playfully tugged her out the door. "Come, my pretty pet. Your hammer awaits."

"Slave driver," she said. Love, a tiny voice in her head corrected her as she followed him into the sunshine. Whatever it was had a name, and that name was love. "No." She didn't know that she had spoken the soft denial aloud.

"Did you say something?" he asked.

"I said, I'll race you down the hill." She pulled her hand out of his and ran ahead. She couldn't bear to touch him another minute, knowing that he was so far away, separated from her by secrets and fences.

He sensed the change in her, and he suspected that she was struggling with the same feelings he had hidden under their light banter. A constraint settled on them as they worked. From time to time Dirk's hammer stilled as he watched Ellen. Although she appeared to be totally involved with the task at hand, she didn't fool him. He saw the tension in her face, felt the strong pull of passion between them. He shouldn't have stayed: He knew that now. But it was too late. He had gone beyond the point of no return. The feelings he had turned loose in Lawrence County had grown beyond his control. He had to have her. It was that simple. That it would be just a summer affair no longer mattered. That he would walk away with her image burned forever into his heart was of no consequence. For a short time Dr. Ellen Stanford would be his. They would have their brief pleasure and handle their parting as two mature adults.

He knew Ellen. He knew the slant of her cheekbones and the tilt of her head. He knew the redgold of her hair in the sunshine and its fiery halo in the moonlight. He could close his eyes and feel the exact shape of her body. He had seen her joy and laughter, her dignity and strength. He *knew* that she could handle anything, even good-bye.

Eight

"Let's call it a day." Dirk put his hammer into the toolbox and stretched. The four o'clock sun was gleaming on his sweat-damp chest. As Ellen glanced up, she decided that Dirk made the male models in suntan ads look positively puny.

"Let's," she agreed. She set her hammer into the toolbox. "I suppose you'll be going back up the mountain."

"It would be more convenient if I stayed here until the work is finished."

She bought time by brushing her hair off her forehead. Was this the same man who always went out of his way to avoid being around her? she wondered. What had happened? "There's an extra room in the main building and also an empty cabin on the compound," she said. "We have overnight guests sometimes—relatives, reporters, visiting scientists."

"The cabin sounds perfect." He looked down at his bedraggled cutoff jeans. "I'll go back to Tony's and toss some things in a bag." He held his hand, palm up, toward her. "Come with me, Ellen."

She looked first at the hand, then deep into his

eyes. The amber light was there again, the same light that had beckoned to her in Lawrenceburg. She knew instinctively that the outstretched hand was more than an invitation to go with Dirk for a change of clothes. She could see it in his eyes. But she had to hear the words. She had to be very sure that what had happened on Uncle Vester's farm would not happen again on Beech Mountain. This time there was no white stallion to carry her away from rejected love.

"Why?" she asked softly.

"I think you know."

"I want to hear you say the words."

His smile was slow and lazy. "Do you want it in writing, Doctor?" The smile took the sting out of the words.

"What would you do if I said yes?"

He reminded her of a lion as he walked toward her, deliberate and purposeful, a golden-hued sleek jungle cat, king of his kind, stalking the victim. She smiled. She had never felt less like a victim in her life. She felt vibrant and alive, and surging with joy.

Dirk didn't stop until he was so close that she could see the tiny scar on his jaw. He cupped her face with his hands, lifting it so that he could look into her eyes. "I would say, 'Get me a piece of paper.'"

She took a long, ragged breath. "You once vowed that you would not be involved in a summer affair."

"Some vows are meant to be broken."

"Are you very sure?"

"Yes." His thumbs traced her jawline as he talked. "I've discovered some things about myself, Ellen."

She smiled. "You said that once too."

"I've discovered feelings that are too strong to be

denied. I've discovered that I have to have you—no matter what the consequences."

The words echoed in her mind: *no matter what the consequences.* It amazed her that she and Dirk were so alike. He had expressed her feelings exactly. She *knew* that her work was a demanding master. She *knew* that a husband and family didn't fit into her plans. Besides that Dirk still had secrets—a name and a past that he had chosen to hide from her. In spite of all that she still wanted him. She wanted to know the touch of his hands on her body. She wanted to know the feel of his lips on her skin.

"Yes," she said. "I'll go with you . . . no matter what the consequences."

It was his turn to ask the question. "You're sure? You're sure you can handle a summer affair with no commitments?"

"Yes." She put her hands over his and pressed them against her face. "I'm very sure."

He leaned down and kissed her lightly. The kiss tasted of sun and pine and sweat salt. It was a miniature lightning bolt, a prelude to the thunderstorm that was to come. He released her lips and took her hand. "Ready, Ellen?"

"As soon as I check on Ruth Ann and Gigi."

Together they walked up the hill. Dirk waited in the shade of a pine tree while Ellen went inside. She found Ruth Ann in the office.

"Is Gigi napping?" Ellen asked.

"Yes. She's been as good as gold today. She knows that she shouldn't have run away." Ruth Ann pushed her glasses down on her nose and studied Ellen. "How's the fence building coming along?"

"We haven't finished. It will probably be at least

another day. Dirk's going to stay in the guest cabin until the job is done."

"Is that necessary? He lives only three miles away."

"No. It isn't necessary, but it's what I want." Ellen spoke quietly. She had already decided that there was no point in trying to keep their affair a secret. She was too old to sneak, and she was too close to her assistant to keep secrets. Besides that Ruth Ann knew everything that went on in the compound. She was nobody's fool.

"You already know what I think," Ruth Ann said. She took her glasses off and polished the already sparkling lenses.

"Yes."

She shoved the glasses back on her nose. "I just hope you know what you're doing, that's all."

"Don't worry about me, Ruth Ann. Dirk and I will be back—"

"There's no need to tell me. I'm not a house mother." Ruth Ann waved toward the door. "Go, go. I'll handle Gigi. You're spoiling her rotten anyhow. She's been trying all day to con me into letting her drive the Buick."

Ellen laughed. "Don't you dare."

"Don't worry. I'm not as softhearted as some people I know."

Ellen left the office and walked into the bright sunlight. Dirk smiled at her.

"Ready, love?" he asked.

"What happened to honey-bunchums?"

He put his arm around her shoulder and led her to his car. "That was for make-believe. This is for real."

As they drove to Tony's cabin, Ellen decided that Beech Mountain had never looked more glorious. It was like a handsome old warrior with rugged, weatherbeaten cheeks of stone, a girdle of stalwart pines, and a victory crown of goldenrod. She thought the setting was altogether appropriate for the beginning of an interlude of pleasure.

Dirk parked Rocinante in the shade by the cabin. "Here we are," he said. He turned and looked at her, his eyes unnaturally bright in the shadows of the car. That was all it took: the simple words and one look.

They didn't know who made the first move, but suddenly they were together in the middle of the seat, holding each other, lips seeking lips, torso straining against torso as they sealed their fate with a kiss.

She tasted the salt of his lips and smelled the wind scent of his hair. Her hands moved restlessly across his bare back until they found what they sought, the jagged scar. Tenderly she traced its lines as her mouth flowered open to welcome his tongue. She moaned at the roughness of his tongue as he caressed the warm satin of her mouth, inciting her body to riot. Their breaths mingled as their tongues danced together, thrusting and probing, a heated prelude to the intimacy to come.

Without the coolness of the air conditioner the car, even under the shade of the pine tree, became a hotbox. Perspiration beaded Ellen's forehead and ran in rivulets between her breasts as she remained locked in Dirk's arms. She could feel his bare chest, sweat-slick and heaving, through the thin cotton of her blouse.

He made a sound deep in his throat and moved his mouth only inches from hers. "I want you, Ellen, but not like this. I want to savor you." Taking her hand, he pulled her almost roughly from the car.

She followed him willingly across the clearing, but as he strode past the cabin she tugged at his hand until he stopped. "Wait." She laughed breathlessly up at him. "Where are we going?"

"I know a place." His voice held the rough edge of suppressed passion. "Follow me."

Right at the moment she would have followed him to the ends of the earth. She smiled at him, and her eyes told him what he needed to know.

Without another word he led her into the woods behind Anthony Salinger's cabin. The trees made a cool canopy over their heads as he guided her to a pond, set like a blue jewel amid the thick growth of pine and oak and willow. Skirting the edge of the pond, they came to a natural bower, walled in by a thick tangle of muscadine vines and a rampant growth of wild roses.

They stopped inside the bower, still holding hands, and looked deep into each other's eyes. All the days of waiting, the lonely hours of wanting, were clearly stamped on their faces. They made no move to embrace but stood perfectly still, savoring the tight moment of anticipation, reveling in the delicious shivers of desire that were running through them.

He reached up slowly to touch the soft tendrils of hair that had slipped from her topknot and framed her face. "All my life I've dreamed of a woman like you and a place like this."

She covered his hand and rubbed it against her cheek. "Do dreams come true?"

"Only when we make them." And Dirk, the man accustomed to the hard knocks and the harsher realities of life, set about making his dream come true.

With a control that he was far from feeling, he let his hands trace the lines of her body, starting at her face, sliding down her neck, moving across her shoulders and down the length of her arms. The hands, sun-bronzed and powerful, moved back up her arms and across her chest, stopping to cup her breasts. Through the fabric of her blouse they teased and molded until her nipples were tight and jutting. She tangled her hands in his dark hair as he lowered his head and opened his mouth over one breast. While his hands continued to knead and mold the other breast, his tongue wet the fabric around her nipple, until the nipple was a dark, tempting rosebud visible through the thin blouse.

Her hands moved in his hair, pulling him closer as her head tipped back. Flashes of heat shot through her body as he took her deep in his mouth. The sensations were heightened by the faint abrasion of wet fabric on her breasts. The heady scent of wild roses filled her nostrils as Dirk moved from one breast to the other, seeking and suckling.

When he at last lifted his head, she was weak-kneed with desire. She felt his hands begin the slow unbuttoning of her blouse.

"I approve this new fashion," he said. His voice was low and hoarse with passion.

"I didn't take time to put on a bra this morning." Her hands moved to his mat of dark chest hair, gold-tipped by the sun. She felt its springy texture as her fingertips explored in erotic circles.

"That's the first thing I noticed this morning," he said, "when you came for Gigi. It's been driving me wild all day." He slid the blouse from her shoulders and let it flutter to the ground. Cupping her face in his hands he urged her closer until their bare chests were touching. His mouth descended on hers, claiming it with hot, wet kisses as he brushed his chest back and forth against hers. Her sensitive nipples, already primed by his tongue, tightened into aching readiness as the crisp hairs of his chest massaged them.

While his mouth slid across hers, wetting her lips, teasing them, tasting them, his hands slipped down to unsnap her shorts. His thumbs hooked the waistband, forcing the shorts to ride low on her hips. She wiggled against him, and the shorts slid down her legs and landed on the grass. He drew her tight against him so that she felt his hardness through the thin silk of her panties.

His hips plunged against hers with growing impatience. He lowered her to the ground and divested himself of his clothes in one fluid movement. The scent of the summer grass and the wild roses seemed to drug her as she felt his hard body on top of her. He rolled to one side, propping himself up on his elbow, and pulled the pins from her hair and flung them aside. With one motion of his powerful hand he loosed her hair and spread it like a flame on the grass.

He bent down and buried his face in her fragrant hair. The silken curls caressed his lips as his hands traveled down her legs, taking the last scrap of clothing that stood between them.

Lifting himself over her, he looked deep into her eyes. "I want you more than I ever dreamed possible," he whispered.

Her head moved restlessly from side to side. "Love me . . . love me, Dirk."

The world tipped sideways as his heavy tumescence slipped into her. He was velvet and she was satin as they began the age-old dance of love. With a tantalizing slowness they moved together in the dappled shadows of the late afternoon sun until the ancient rhythm became a frenzied beat. The sun shot from the sky and melted inside Ellen as

Dirk became jagged lightning and rolling thunder. Her shoulders pushed into the grass as she met the fury of his storm with an abandon that matched his.

His hoarse cry filled the bower as they rode out the storm together. She arched high for his powerful thrusts, her hands clenched on his tense back and her head thrown back in the fragrant grass. Her body shuddered with completion as he drenched her with the final fury of his love.

Their limp legs tangled together as he lay on top of her, spent. His cheek rested in her hair and his damp chest pressed against her breasts.

"Ellen?" His voice was muffled by her hair.

"Hmm?"

"I'm already wishing the summer would last forever."

"So am I."

They stayed locked together, not speaking, until the lowering sun began to pink the western horizon, and he slipped, unbidden, from her. He rolled off her and raised himself to his knees, pulling her up with him.

"Follow me, love." He held out his hand.

As she reached out she teased, "You're always saying that."

He pulled her to her feet. "I've always wanted to have a beautiful woman do my bidding."

"Just any woman?"

"No. Only the red-haired ones."

"Which red-haired ones?"

"The ones who live on Beech Mountain and teach gorillas to talk." Without warning he scooped her into his arms. Looking down into her face, he spoke earnestly. "Only the one whose hair smells like wild flowers and whose body makes a man forget."

"Forget what?" Her green eyes searched his black ones for answers.

As the sun sank lower and the scent of wild roses became more pronounced on the still evening air, Dirk lowered one more barrier. "The evil that men do," he said. "The reasons for prisons and wars." His eyes became blacker than night as he added one last bit of truth to the revelation. "The reason for my loneliness."

She reached up and gently touched the tiny scar on his jaw. "I'm glad I could make you forget."

He shrugged his shoulders as if the motion could cast off the real world. Suddenly he laughed, startling a pair of cardinals into flight. "Time's a-wastin'." He strode swiftly to the pond.

"You sound like Aunt Lollie," she said.

"Where do you think I learned that expression? That woman has a way with words."

As he put his foot into the water she realized his intent. "Dirk! It'll be cold. Even in summer these mountain ponds are chilly."

"Where's your sense of adventure?" He waded farther into the water until he was standing thigh-deep. He lowered his arms briefly, dipping her backside into the cold water.

"Dirk Smith Caldwell the Third! Put me down."

"Benedict," he said calmly as he dumped her into the water.

She came up sputtering and gasping, but the shock of the cool water was nothing compared to the shock of hearing his name. Tossing her wet hair out of her eyes, she stared at him. "Benedict? For real?"

He nodded. "Benedict." Turning from her, he arched his body and dived cleanly into the water. With strong strokes he swam toward the middle of the lake.

"Come back here," she yelled. "You can't just leave it at that."

"Come and get me," he shouted. Grinning wickedly, he went underwater again.

With the blood thrumming in her ears with this new knowledge and her body still ablaze with recent lovemaking, Ellen decided that the pond was not too cold after all. She jackknifed expertly into the water and swam after him.

Suddenly she felt her left foot being tugged. Even under the water Dirk's hand sent shivers up her leg. She took a deep breath before she was pulled under. His hands slid up her body, inch by inch, until he was clasping her around the waist.

The water distorted his features and played with his thick, dark hair. With his hands guiding her she floated closer until their bodies were touching, length to length. He lowered his head for an aquatic kiss, a brief skimming of lip across lip, and then, holding her tight, he shot to the surface.

Ellen shook her hair from her eyes. "So. You like to play games, do you?" She reached out and ducked him.

Instead of coming back up, he grabbed her ankle again and pulled her under. Reflections from the sunset sky turned their bodies to gold as they cavorted like two of nature's children. Their combined laughter rang out in the still air, and its happy sound was so right, so much a part of nature, that the two deer who had come to the edge of the pond for a quiet evening drink simply lifted their heads for a moment and, finding nothing to alarm, continued their drinking.

Refreshed from the swim and invigorated by laughter, Ellen and Dirk joined hands and of one accord waded to the shallow edge of the pond. He stopped when they were knee-deep and looked down at her. Lifting one finger he traced the edge of her cheekbone and the line of her jaw.

"So beautiful," he murmured. "You are so beautiful." Bending down, he followed the path of his hands with his tongue, licking away the droplets of water on her face. His lips found the hollow of her throat and paused there, pressed against the soft skin that fluttered from the sudden wild thumping of her heart.

Joy flooded her as he lifted her from the water and carried her ashore. Their private bower was now shadowed with purple and redolent with the scent of roses.

He stood, looking into her face. "I love these mountains," he said. What he wanted to say was *I love you.*

"I will always remember the smell of wild roses," she murmured. What she wanted to say was *I will always remember you.*

He lowered her to the grass, letting her wet body slide against his. By the time her feet touched the ground, she was aware of his pulsing shaft and her own growing passion. Their arms locked, and they held each other fiercely, not kissing but letting their bodies communicate their mutual need.

The grass welcomed them as they sank to the ground, and they rolled over and over, feeling, bumping, touching, not wanting to let go. Not ever wanting to let go.

At last they stopped, and Dirk lay on top of Ellen, breathing harshly. He slipped to her side and gently brushed away the bits of grass that clung to her still-wet body. His touch sent shivers skittering along her spine, and she arched toward his hand.

Without speaking, he let his fingers trail across her breasts. His face filled with pleasure at the instant response. Lowering his head, he took the ripe tips between his teeth and tugged gently. Ellen buried her face in his hair and knew the return of splendor.

His mouth and tongue feasted on the heavy, love-filled treasures until she was writhing beneath his touch. He parted her legs and moved his questing mouth downward. His tongue left a path of liquid fire in its wake. He explored the indentation of her navel, the soft downy fuzz on her stomach, the satin of her inner thighs. And when his tongue nudged its way into the dark triangle between her legs, spasms of ecstasy ripped through her.

When she became limp under his expert lovemaking, he rolled to his back and pulled her on top of him, fitting her over his hard shaft. The world seemed to explode as she was once more caught up in the frenzy of passion.

Time stood still for Ellen and Dirk as their bodies spoke love on top of Beech Mountain. They both told themselves that this was a grand beginning of a summer affair, but deep inside they knew better. Theirs was a joining that claimed the heart as surely as any vows ever spoken. Theirs was a coming together of two lonely people, the bonding of two brilliant deceivers who experienced love while denying its existence.

The moon was riding high when they left the bower, replete. Clutching their rumpled clothes in their hands, they walked through the moonlight to Anthony's cabin.

Dirk held open the door for her. "There's no need to return to the compound tonight," he said.

"No need," she agreed.

"The car might disturb them."

"They're probably already asleep."

"Do you want the light?" he asked. The cabin

was flooded with the light of a full moon that poured through the enormous skylight in the center of the room.

"How can you improve on nature?" she said.

His eyes sparkled as his gaze raked her body. "Impossible," he agreed. "Nature outdid herself." He took a step toward her.

She lifted her hands, laughing. "Dirk! Don't you ever get hungry?"

"Only for you." He leaned over and nipped her neck.

Pretending impatience with him, she crossed her arms on her bare breasts. "Are you going to feed me or do I have to steal Rocinante and make my escape down the mountain?"

"You distract the cook." He walked to a closet and pulled out a blue denim shirt. "Here," he said, tossing it to her. "Put this on or we'll never get around to food."

She caught the shirt deftly and headed for the shower. Anthony's cabin was almost as familiar to her as her own. He had been her friend and confidant since she had moved to Beech Mountain. "Don't fix eggs," she called over her shoulder. "I hate eggs."

Dirk fixed them anyway. He had many skills, but cooking was not one of them. His hale and hearty body was not a tribute to his cooking, but rather to his habits of exercising and eating natural foods.

When Ellen returned from the shower, Dirk's shirt buttoned low, exposing the tops of her breasts, she saw the table was set with a platter of fresh fruits—peeled oranges, sliced apples, bananas, and bunches of grapes—a loaf of whole wheat bread, and a platter of eggs.

Dirk, dressed in a clean pair of faded cutoff jeans, pulled back her chair. "Welcome to this humble repast," he said. He captured her hand and kissed the inside of her wrist before sitting down at the other side of the table.

"Eggs!" she said.

"My specialty." He dished up a generous helping. "What's yours?" He grinned wickedly at her. "Cooking, I mean."

"I'm a scientist. I don't cook," she said serenely as she helped herself to the fruit. "Why do you think God invented Betty Crocker and Sara Lee?"

He chuckled. "It's a good thing we don't plan a permanent liaison. We'd starve to death."

"A very good thing," she said, but the words had the hollow ring of falsehood and the fruit in her mouth turned to sawdust. She propped her elbows on Anthony's glass-top table. It was best not to talk about things like permanence and commitment, she decided. They were mutually exclusive with brief affairs. "How do you know Tony?" she asked. A nice, safe topic, she thought. One guaranteed not to cause racing pulses and crazy thoughts.

"Tony and I met in Spain—on the Costa del Sol." Dirk laughed, remembering. "His yacht was moored in a harbor at Malaga. We had both come in from a day's fishing. He was empty-handed and I had a catch big enough to feed half the population of Spain. I shared my fish, and we've been fast friends ever since. He's a remarkable man."

"So he is. Not many men can make their first million before the age of thirty and retire at forty-five." She glanced around the cabin. Its rustic exterior was deceiving. Modern chrome-and-glass furniture, plush white throw rugs, Chinese porcelain, and carved jade accessories all reflected the expensive tastes of its owner. Ellen turned her attention back to Dirk. She knew why Tony had been in Spain: He went where whim carried him.

But what about Dirk? Would she learn one more tidbit to fit into the jigsaw puzzle of his life? "Why were you in Spain?" she asked.

"Would you believe me if I told you I was living in another convent, posing as a nun?"

"No."

"I thought not." He looked out the window into the darkened woods. His hands paused in the act of breaking a piece of brown bread, and he seemed to be struggling to come to a decision. Abruptly he turned back to her. "I was there on business."

Ellen had not even been aware that she was holding her breath. It came out in a relieved whoosh. First his real name and now his work, she exulted. It seemed that tonight she had hit the jackpot. "And what kind of business is that, Dirk Benedict?" she asked softly.

His black-as-doom eyes sparkled as he slowly put down his bread and reached across the table. He captured both her hands and turned them over, letting his thumbs trace the pale network of blue veins on the inside of her wrists. "I have a confession to make," he said.

"What?" She scarcely breathed.

"There's something I've been wanting to tell you for a long time." His thumbs continued their sensuous circling.

Would it explain the scar? she wondered. Would it explain his reticence? "You can tell me anything."

Still holding her hands, he stood up and walked around the table. Pulling her up beside him, he tipped her face so that he could look deep into her eyes. "You have grape juice in the most provocative place."

"Oh, you . . ." She started to vent her frustration that he had once again hidden behind his wall of secrecy, but his head dipped toward hers, and she felt his tongue flick the side of her mouth. Her frustration changed to pleasure as the touch sent shivers down her spine.

"Hmm, nice," he said against her skin. "I've always wanted to have a loaf of bread, a bunch of grapes, and you."

"I think that's 'a loaf of bread, a jug of wine, and—' "

"Hush," he murmured as his lips moved across hers. "This is my fantasy."

The kiss was silk against silk, feather-light and provocative. She felt the familiar fire that only Dirk could kindle begin deep in her loins and inflame her body. She wound her hands in his hair as he pushed her back against the edge of the table and reached behind her.

Holding her hips to his with one hand pressed against the small of her back, he lifted his head. "I've always wanted to have my grapes this way." He moved his head toward the bunch of white grapes in his free hand. With one deft motion he plucked a grape with his teeth.

Taking her cue, Ellen lifted her lips toward the tantalizing fruit in his mouth. "Hmm," she murmured as their lips meet and the sweet juice squirted into their mouths. The kiss lasted until not a trace of juice was left.

Ellen cocked her head to one side. "There's something I've been wanting to tell you all evening," she said teasingly.

"What's that, my love?"

"I've always wanted to do a scientific study on the correlation between grapes and sexual pleasure." She plucked a grape with her mouth and stood on tiptoe to place it on the shelf of his shoulder between his neck and his collarbone.

He stood very still as she bit the grape and traced the tiny trail of juice with her tongue. That questing tongue sent surges of pleasure ripping through him, and he wondered why he had denied the pleasure for so long. Her hot tongue moved across his chest, far beyond the reaches of the grape juice, and her hips began a rhythmic cadence against his own.

Unable to restrain himself any longer, he lifted her and carried her to the plush white rug in the center of the cabin. The moonlight streaming through the skylight turned her hair to flame as he laid her down. Leaning over her, he unfastened the top button of the blue work shirt and placed a grape between her breasts. "Between my fantasy and your scientific analysis," he said, "this could take a long time."

"A very long time," she said. He lowered his head, and she shivered with delight when she felt the small rivulet of juice run between the valley of her breasts.

"Doctor, I love your fruit," he murmured against her moon-silvered skin as his lips and tongue followed the path of the juice.

"I can't draw . . . a conclusion . . . until all . . . the data . . . is in." She spoke between sharp gasps of ecstasy.

And those were the last words uttered until the grapes were gone and the fantasy had ended. Only the moon was witness to what they did with the grapes, and if Ellen had ever decided to publish her findings, nobody would have believed her.

At last, redolent with the sweet scent of grapes and the pungent scent of love, they retired to Tony's enormous brass bed and fell into exhausted sleep.

* * *

Ellen stirred in her sleep and pressed herself closer to Dirk's back. In the semidarkness of predawn, she became aware of sound. It was a soft agonized moan. Years of round-the-clock research with Gigi made her instantly alert.

Dirk flung his arm out and groaned again. It was a half-articulated "No," a denial of the dark things that haunted his dreams.

Ellen placed her lips on the scar slanting across his back and tenderly rubbed her hand across his shoulder. "Hush, love," she crooned. Another anguished sound escaped his lips. She wrapped both arms around him and gently rocked. "It's all right, Dirk. It's all right." She spoke softly, soothingly, holding and rocking him until his restlessness stilled and his breathing became an easy rise and fall of his chest.

Lifting herself on her elbow, she looked down at him. "What demons haunt you, my love?" she whispered. "What is the secret that keeps you locked away from me?"

She lay back against the pillow and closed her eyes, but sleep evaded her. She stared through the skylight at the first pink of morning and rose quietly from the brass bed. Padding barefoot to the white rug, she retrieved Dirk's shirt and shrugged into it. The latch of the door clicked faintly behind her.

The splinters on the porch pricked her bare bottom as she sat and looked out across the vista of Beech Mountain. Nature was putting on another glorious display as it gave birth to a new day. The dew on the grass took on the jeweled hues of rare diamonds, and the songbirds outdid themselves inventing new arias to welcome the day. The still morning air was heady with the mingled perfumes of mountain wild flowers.

Ellen hugged her knees to her chest. Her affair was only one day old, and already she could feel the lonesomeness of the parting. Already she knew that the man lying on Anthony Salinger's enormous brass bed inside the cabin was more to her than a fake fiancé. He was also more to her than a passing fancy. He was the other half of herself. He was the one man who could fill the void in her heart. Out of all the men in the world, Dirk Benedict, man of mystery and deceit, was the only one who could make her life complete.

"A pretty pickle you've gotten yourself into, Dr. Ellen Stanford," she scolded herself. "You should have stuck to gorilla research and left the grapes to somebody else." She sighed. She didn't know love could hurt so much.

Nine

Dirk and Ellen spent the next few glorious days alternating between building the fence and building their relationship. That the fence took six days to build, instead of the projected two, spoke eloquently of their preoccupation with each other.

Part of Dirk's belongings were in the guest cabin on the compound and part of them were still in Tony's cabin. Ellen and Dirk whizzed giddily up and down the mountain, following whims and the urgings of their flesh. The white rug, the brass bed, the rose bower beside the lake, and the spool bed on the compound all became special places of delight. Often the ringing of their hammers would cease before the sun had reached its noonday brightness. All it took between them was one look, and they would join hands and disappear into the summer day.

Ruth Ann accepted the affair with stoic silence, and Gigi accepted Dirk's presence with outrageous displays of joy. Ellen taught Dirk the signs that Gigi used, and a bond of genuine affection was forged between man and gorilla. Whenever she saw them together, Ellen would again feel something akin to envy. Nothing was held back with the gorilla. Gigi constantly signed *love* with her hands, while Ellen could only sign *love* with her heart. Though they were on the mountaintop, miles removed from civilization, she could not put aside civilized restraints. Dirk had set the boundaries for the affair—no commitments—and she would not be the first one to cross the line.

The sun-filled, love-filled days of June and July slipped by. Ellen and Dirk pretended not to notice their passing. They deceived themselves into thinking the summer would go on forever. But August came, and with it a thunderstorm. Ellen stood at the window of the guest cabin on the compound and watched nature lash Beech Mountain with her fury. What was Dirk thinking? she wondered, as she watched the play of lightning in the night sky. He had been brooding and tense all day, and not even their lovemaking had dispelled her feeling that he was a keg of gunpowder, set to explode.

Half turning from the window, she spoke over her shoulder. "The storm reminds me of you."

He leaned back against the pillows and pretended a nonchalance he didn't feel. His mind swung back to the letter he had received—his new assignment. His palms became damp, and he felt a familiar surge of excitement that he would once more be embroiled in the life-and-death adventure of battling evil. He gazed at the woman at the window, and the excitement became tinged with sadness. The job he loved was waiting, but Ellen made going back hard. "In what way, love?" he asked. His light question was a masterpiece of deception, an elaborate pretense that the summer would never end. But Ellen knew him too well.

She turned fully from the window so that she

could face him. "Both of you are charged with power."

He smiled, and it, too, was a masterpiece of deception. "Come back to bed, love. I'll show you power."

She locked her hands behind her back, forcing herself not to run into the safe haven of his arms, where questions didn't exist and answers didn't matter. "It's more than the power—" She stopped, watching his face. Although the smile stayed in place, the black eyes showed caution. "It's the violence." The face didn't change.

She walked across the room and sat on the edge of the bed. Putting her hand on his back, she let her fingers trail the bronze skin until she found what she sought. "Tell me about the scar, Dirk." She rubbed her fingertips along its jagged edge.

He sat very still for a moment, letting the feel of her hands and the nearness of her body seep into his turmoiled spirit. "Ahh, Ellen." Winding his arms tightly around her, he crushed her against his chest. "Do you know how good you are for me? Do you have any idea what this summer has meant?"

"Tell me." Her voice was muffled against his shoulder.

"You've given me a sense of place and a sense of family. I feel almost as if Beech Mountain were my home."

It could be, she wanted to say. Instead, she remained silent, waiting for him to continue.

"I have no family, Ellen, and my home was always whichever orphanage would take a rambunctious boy who was too much trouble to be adopted."

"Then you were telling the truth that first day on my front porch?"

"I've always told you the truth"—he lifted his head to grin crookedly at her—"more or less."

She cupped his face and rubbed her cheek against his jaw. "Less than more, I think."

"The government gave me a chance to belong, to be a part of something, even if it was only a system."

She sucked her breath in sharply, and a feeling of foreboding filled her heart. She put her fingers over his lips. "Shh. You don't have to say any more, Dirk."

He kissed her fingertips and removed her hand. "I think I do. It's time—past time—for you to know the truth."

"No." She shook her head, and her green eyes widened. Outside the storm battered the roof and assaulted the windows. Lightning ripped the dark sky and thunder ricocheted off the mountains. Her emotions rivaled the storm. "Summer's almost over," she said. "You'll be gone. Let's just leave the mystery."

"It's become important to me that you know why I must go." He looked deep into her eyes. "I work for the CIA, Ellen."

She let out a long, ragged breath. Sometimes, she thought, there's more hope in mystery than in the truth. If he had gone, shrouded in mystery, she could have pretended that he would change his mind and come back. But not now. Now she knew. She knew about the scar. She knew about the "no commitments" policy. She knew about the feeling of power and violence that surrounded him.

She leaned her forehead against his neck. Her demons suddenly seemed pussycats compared to his.

"The scar is a souvenir of my job," he continued. "I was working undercover in Casablanca when it happened." He squeezed her tightly. "Danger is a part of my life. Violence is my constant companion." His lips brushed her hair back from her forehead. "I could never ask anyone to share that with me."

She squeezed him as if she would never let go. She willed time to stand still, but she could hear autumn, wearing stormtrooper boots, coming in on the heels of the rain. So much loving and so little time. She squeezed again. He was as implacable as Beech Mountain. It was, she thought, foolish to waste time arguing that she could share anything as long as it was with him. She lifted her head and looked at him with false brightness. "Mr. Dirk Benedict, are we involved in a summer affair or in a dreary discussion?" She leaned down and playfully nipped his neck. "Time's a-wastin'."

He smiled and took her with all the passion of the storm outside. Theirs was a fierce joining without tenderness, a desperate coming together that sought to deny endings.

Everything changed after that night. It was almost as if Ellen and Dirk had already said good-bye. Their last two weeks together were blurred, like a movie reel run too fast. And they continued the gay deceit, right to the very end.

"Special delivery for Dr. Ellen Stanford." Ellen's white lab coat flared as she spun around at the sound of the voice. Her concentration on her work had been so intense that she had not heard a vehicle drive up. A delivery boy was standing in the doorway, his face hidden behind an enormous bouquet of yellow-throated orchids.

She pulled her glasses off and put them on her desk beside the report she had been updating. If she had been Gigi, she thought, she would have turned a somersault in delight. But she was Dr. Ellen Stanford. She tilted her elegant head to one side, studying the bouquet and wondering if this was Dirk's way of saying good-bye.

"Sign here," the boy said.

She signed for the flowers and waited until she heard the engine of the departing truck before she opened the card. *The fish weren't biting,* the card read. *Tuck a flower behind your ear, put on your dancing shoes, and Ill see you at eight.*

"So I'm playing second fiddle to a fish," she said as she searched her office for a container large enough to hold the flowers, but she was smiling. There were too many orchids for one vase. By the time she had finished arranging them, her office looked like a hothouse.

"Has somebody died?" Ruth Ann asked dryly. "This place looks like a jungle." She picked her way around the flowers. "Can't even find the desk," she grumbled.

"The flowers are from Dirk."

Ruth Ann looked at Ellen's flushed cheeks and the flower tucked behind her ear. "I didn't think they were from Santa Claus," she said, and picked up the report Ellen had been updating. "Crazy man. Nothing's been the same around here since he came." She plucked her glasses off and began to polish the spotless lenses, a sure sign that she was upset.

Ellen sat down on the edge of the desk and covered the report with her hand. "Let's talk, Ruth Ann."

"I'm listening."

"You don't like Dirk, do you?"

"I didn't say that." Ruth Ann shoved the glasses

back on her nose. "Didn't say that at all. As a matter of fact, he's quite a likable man."

Ellen smiled. "Gigi thinks so, too, and I've never known her to be wrong in her judgment of character."

"And what about you? What do you think?"

"I think"—she bit back the witty reply that had been on the tip of her tongue—"I think that I'm in love with him. I think that I want him to stay on Beech Mountain forever. And I think that I've probably taken leave of my senses."

"That's what I was afraid of." Ruth Ann made a careful pyramid of her fingertips. "I've felt it since he first set foot on this compound. Old maid that I am, I'm not immune to romance going on right under my nose."

"He'll be leaving soon."

"I've known that all along too. There's a burr under that man's saddle, and he won't sit still until somebody plucks it out." Ruth Ann cleared her throat self-consciously. "Why do you think I've hated having him around? I didn't want to see you hurt."

"Life's full of ironic twists, isn't it? I fell in love with a fiancé of my own making. I'm caught in my own web of duplicity."

"If you need a shoulder to cry on, I'm here." Ruth Ann gave her a grim smile. "It's bony and hasn't been used in a number of years, but it's there." She hurried from the room, but not before Ellen saw the telltale moisture behind her glasses.

Ellen selected her dress carefully, a bright yellow linen with full skirt, plunging neckline, and thin straps, just right for dancing. She had to pull it from the back of the closet, and as she did a small stuffed animal tumbled off the shelf and landed at her feet. It was a yellow bear with one button eye and most of his fuzz missing.

Clutching the dress in her hand, she knelt and scooped up the tattered toy. "Pooh Bear," she said softly. "Hello, old friend." She pressed the souvenir of her past against her cheek.

The bear stared placidly back at her, his lopsided grin still intact, and she remembered the wonderful days of her childhood—the spicy smell of Aunt Lollie's gingerbread, the cozy sound of corn popping on a cold winter's day, and the feel of the sun on her back as she lay in the hayloft daydreaming, Pooh Bear at her side.

Carefully she set him on her dressing table. "It seems I've spent too little time these last few years dancing and daydreaming," she mused aloud as she slipped the yellow dress over her head. She left her hair loose and pinned an orchid in the shining red tresses. "What do you think, Pooh Bear?" She spun around for his inspection. "Remember that prince I used to dream about, the one who would ride a white charger? He's coming tonight." She picked up the stuffed bear and rubbed his scruffy stomach. "The only problem is, he doesn't want to be a prince."

Ruth Ann tapped politely on her door, then poked her head into the room. "Is somebody in here with you?" she asked.

"No. I just found my old friend, Pooh Bear. His ears are tattered, but he's a good listener."

"While you were renewing old acquaintance with your stuffed toy, somebody came to the door."

"Dirk!"

"Who were you expecting? Herbert Hoover?"

Ellen whizzed out the door, and if she had turned back around she would have fainted. Ruth

Ann actually had a smile on her face. It was a sad smile, tinged with nostalgia, but still, it was a smile. "I hope she remembers this bony old shoulder, Pooh Bear," Ruth Ann said softly. "She's going to need it." Her sensible shoes clicked against the floor as she hurried out of the room. "Lord, just listen to me. Talking to myself. I've been on this mountain too long."

"Orchids become you," Dirk said. He was leaning against the door, looking impossibly handsome in an Italian-made shirt of raw silk and fawn-colored pants that seemed designed to show off his muscular legs.

"More than grapes?" Ellen asked. She moved quickly to him and put her hands on his shoulders.

"Not more than grapes." He grasped her waist and pulled her close. "Never more than grapes," he said as he bent down to claim her lips.

"It seems like years," she said when they came up for air.

"Is it my fault you didn't come fishing today, Doctor?"

"I have to keep up the appearance of working." As he escorted her to the car, she reached up and touched his lips. "Even if my mind was on the fish."

"Is that what you're calling it now? Fish?"

"Did anybody ever tell you that you have a bawdy tongue?"

"Why do you think I kept getting shuffled off to so many different orphanages? A bad influence, I was called." There was no rancor in his voice. He even laughed when he said it.

She slid across the seat and put her head on his

shoulder. "Well, I call you wonderful. Did I thank you properly for the orchids?"

"You thanked me properly. What I'm hoping for is an improper thank-you."

"Like I said . . . a bawdy tongue."

They kept the banter going all the way down the mountain. Dirk turned left on Beech Mountain Parkway and drove to the Beech Haus. "This should make a nice change from my eggs," he said once they were seated.

"Actually I've grown quite fond of your eggs."

"Not to mention my grapes."

She delicately kicked him. "Is that any way to behave in a proper restaurant?" she whispered.

"It's better than what I'm thinking of doing in this proper restaurant."

"I wouldn't touch that statement with a ten-foot pole." She hid her smile behind the menu.

The waitress recommended their Bavarian chicken soup, and as Ellen placed her order she felt Dirk's foot creep up her leg. "Soup" came out "coop," and she had a coughing fit to cover her laughter. By the time she got to the potato pancakes, his foot had wormed its way under her skirt and was sending indecent shivers up her thigh. Her face was as red as her hair from suppressing her laughter, and she heard herself tell the poor confused waitress that she wanted grape strudel for dessert.

"I'm sorry, ma'am, but apple is the only kind of strudel we have."

Dirk straightened the whole thing out, cool as a cucumber, Ellen thought, just as if his toes weren't busy kneading the insides of her thigh.

After the waitress left, Ellen leaned across the table. "Thank goodness for long tablecloths."

"Thank goodness for warm, sweet thighs."

"Grape strudel, indeed! Look what you've done to me."

"You should see what you've done to me." He grinned wickedly.

"It's those damn toes."

"It's that sexy yellow dress."

"Remove your toes."

"If you'll remove that dress."

She felt exhilarated. He was the old Dirk again, arrogant and totally outrageous. For the moment the CIA and summer's end were forgotten.

In their darkened corner she leaned against the back of her padded booth and casually let one strap slide from her shoulder. "Now?" she asked softly.

"After the chicken soup," he said calmly. But he removed his foot.

They made it a leisurely meal, savoring the food and each other.

"Mmm, delicious," she said of the soup. But her eyes said it of Dirk.

"Wonderful," he pronounced the pancakes, but his gaze was locked on Ellen.

They shared the strudel. Prolonging the intimate dessert, she broke off tiny pieces and put them into his mouth. He nibbled her sugared fingers as his dark eyes held hers across the candlelit table. Every touch of her fingers was a knife wound in his heart, for tomorrow he would be leaving. "I love you," his eyes tried to tell her, and he hoped that she understood.

After the meal they climbed into Rocinante and Dirk drove back up Beech Mountain.

"I thought we were going dancing," Ellen said.

"We are."

"Where?"

"Trust me."

"I already did that once tonight, and what did I get? Chicken coop and grape strudel."

"That's what you get for being a bawdy woman."

"Ha! Look who's talking." She pressed her head into the curve of his shoulder and thought, *That's what I get for being a woman in love*. She didn't even lift her head when they passed the compound. She knew where they were going.

Dirk parked the car in front Tony's cabin. "Here we are, love. A private club."

"My favorite night spot."

He helped her from the car. "Did anyone ever tell you that you're brilliant, Doctor?" Pulling her against him, he nuzzled her hair.

"Only Gigi," she said, "and I'm not sure she's to be trusted."

I'm even going to miss that gorilla, Dirk thought. Taking Ellen's hand, he urged her inside. "Come, love. The orchestra awaits."

"I hope they're wearing blinders. I've always fancied dancing in the nude."

Dirk's laughter startled a screech owl in the pine tree beside Tony's porch. "Is that any way for a sweet Southern belle to talk? We Connecticut Yankees have delicate sensibilities."

"I've never been sweet a day in my life, and if you're delicate, I'm a monkey's uncle."

"A monkey's mother," he retorted, kicking the door shut behind him. He looked down at her and suddenly the teasing stopped. "Ahh, Ellen." He pulled her into his arms and held her tightly against his chest.

She clung to his broad shoulders, rubbing her cheek against the roughness of his raw silk shirt. "Start the music, Dirk," she said.

And he did.

"Is this a new kind of dancing?" she asked.

"Yes." His lips nudged her straps aside and seared the tops of her breasts. Her skirt made a bright splash of yellow as he lowered her to the rug. Leaning over her, he let his hands trace her legs through the dress. "You look like a bright yellow daffodil." His hands moved up her body, following the indentation of her waist and the shape of her breasts. "This is called 'The Waltz of the Flowers.' "

She smiled. "I think that's already been done."

"Not the way I plan to do it." He stretched out beside her and pulled her into his arms.

"Innovation is your strong point," she agreed as their gazes locked and held in the moonlit room. She felt his hand on her zipper and heard the metallic whisper as he lowered it, inch by sensuous inch, letting his fingers caress her skin in its widening path.

"Is that a scientific observation, Doctor?" he asked. Both hands were on her bare back now, doing magic things to her skin as he pushed the dress aside.

"No. It's a personal preference." She popped open the first button on his shirt and moved her hands inside. The dark springy hairs on his chest curled around her fingers in possession.

"This waltz could take a long time," he said thickly as he lowered his head.

"A very long time," she murmured while there was still time to talk. And then they were caught up in the ancient waltz of love, lost in the music of their own making.

Afterward they lay on the rug, arms and legs still entwined, looking up through the skylight.

"Summer's almost gone," he said quietly.

"Yes." An ominous feeling overcame her. Her arms tightened around him.

"I'll be leaving tomorrow."

She had been dreading this moment since the first of August. She had known the end was coming. Even so, her chest felt so constricted that she could hardly breathe. "So this is good-bye?"

"No. I don't like good-byes."

"Neither do I."

They held each other in silence and watched the moon track across the sky.

"It's been a beautiful interlude," he said finally. His tongue felt too thick for his mouth, and he wondered why the words were so hard to say. He *did* hate good-byes, especially this one. He wanted to plunge into the dark forest and howl his loneliness like a wolf. He wanted to bang his fist against a tree and curse the Fates who had made their union impossible. For the first time in his life he resented the element of danger in his job, a danger that precluded intimate relationships. Life was full of twists of fate, he thought. The thing he found most intriguing about his work—the danger, the excitement of pitting his own cunning against those who threatened his country, the freedom of others—was what stood between him and Ellen. There was too much risk. He couldn't endanger the woman he loved. There. He had finally admitted it. Love. That special something he had sought in his early life and run from in his adult life had finally caught up with him. He loved Dr. Ellen Stanford, and that made the parting all the more sorrowful.

"Yes," she said while her heart broke in two. "A beautiful interlude."

He kissed her damp forehead and thought how he would miss her. He wanted to say *I love you*, but he dared not. He clenched his jaw against the words.

"Did you say something?" she asked.

"No." He rubbed his cheek against hers. First

there had been the parade of orphanages that had made permanent ties with friends and even pets impossible, and now this. His work. Was it possible, he wondered, that Ellen had the strength to deal with his job? He quickly squelched the thought. It wouldn't be fair to ask someone else to share the danger. He held her tightly, and the agony of choice threatened to break him. He had never dreamed that once he found love it would be so hard to let go.

He wanted to say, *I can never let you go, Ellen.* Instead, he said, "Is it all right if I stop by the compound tomorrow to see Gigi before I go?"

"I think you should," she said. "I'll let her know you're coming." Gigi will vent her feelings, she thought. She won't hide her heartbreak under polite conversation and a brave smile.

Dirk turned to her and looked deep into her eyes. "Ellen." That's all he said, just her name. But his voice was haunted with all the loneliness of his past and all the lonesome times of his future.

They came together in a frenzy of passion that sought to hold back time. But nature kept her appointments, and when the last star was dimmed by the approaching sun, Dirk took Ellen back to the compound.

Ellen stood outside the new fence, watching Dirk and Gigi say good-bye. The bright August sun beat down on them, wilting the goldenrod bouquet Gigi was clutching tightly in her hand. The gorilla's face was solemn as she watched Dirk sign and speak.

"I have to go, Gigi."

She put the bouquet on top of her head and

asked with her hands, *Man go see brothers and sisters?*

"No," Dirk signed. "Go to work. Go to big city."

Where big city?

"Far away."

Gigi come too.

"No. I'm sorry, Gigi. I must go alone."

No. Gigi come. Her face lit up with sudden inspiration. *Gigi drive!*

Ellen covered her mouth to keep from laughing. She noticed that Dirk was also struggling to suppress his mirth.

He reached out and patted the gorilla's face. "Gigi must stay. Ellen needs Gigi."

Gigi swung her massive head around to look at Ellen. Her bright eyes snapped with intelligence as she looked back at Dirk. *Ellen brave,* she signed. *Ellen stay alone. Gigi go.*

"I'm sorry, Gigi. I must go alone. Work hard. No women can go."

No fine animal gorillas? Gigi stuck out her lower lip.

"No fine animal gorillas."

Gigi have sad heart.

Dirk touched Gigi's heart and then touched his own. "Man have sad heart too. Good-bye, Gigi."

Ellen watched as Gigi accepted the farewell. The gorilla lifted her hand in a solemn wave as Dirk strode from the summer enclosure.

Dirk hurried toward his car, bent on putting the mountain compound out of sight as quickly as possible. Out of sight, out of mind, he hoped. But his footsteps slowed when he saw Ellen standing beside the fence.

He lifted his hand, intending a brief wave and a hasty departure, but he could no more have passed her by than he could have flown to the moon. He strode quickly to her. Without speaking, he pulled her into his arms for a fierce kiss.

A world of unspoken vows was in that kiss, and when it was over, he lifted his head and looked into her eyes.

"Take care, Ellen," he said gruffly.

"Be safe," she whispered. And then he was gone.

He waited until he was halfway down the mountain before giving vent to his feelings. "Damn!" he exploded. Instead of going back to his job with a renewed sense of purpose, he was going back reluctantly. More than reluctantly, he corrected himself. For the first time since he had taken this job, he didn't feel a surge of excitement at pitting himself against the evils of the world. He didn't welcome danger as a means of keeping his world free. His knuckles turned white as he gripped the steering wheel and negotiated the sharp mountain curves. Ellen's face was everywhere he looked—in the waving branches of pine, in the majestic sweep of the mountains, in the lonesome stretches of the road. And he knew, as surely as he knew his own name, that he could never escape her. Though he put thousands of miles between them, she was forever emblazoned on his heart.

Ten

Dirk unstrapped his gun and tossed it onto the bed. Rubbing his forehead wearily, he crossed to the window. Everthing looked the same. The Washington Monument was still there. The pigeons searching for crumbs on his windowsill were still there. The difference was not in his surroundings but in himself, he thought. His body was in Washington, D.C., but his heart was still in the mountains of North Carolina.

He smacked his fist against the windowsill, then turned and headed for the shower. It had been a long, tiring day. And it wasn't over yet. The summer of indulgence had taken its toll. He still had a hundred push-ups to do before the day was over.

He was halfway to the shower when the buzzer announced a visitor. He switched on the intercom.

"Open the door, you handsome rascal," Anthony Salinger's voice boomed over the intercom. "I have a fish story to tell."

Dirk chuckled. "Come on up, you scruffy old vagabond."

Within minutes Tony was stepping out of the security elevator and into Dirk's apartment. The old friends clasped hands and shoulders and grinned at each other.

Dirk's gaze swept over Tony's shock of thick hair, prematurely white; his pale blue eyes, set in a network of suntanned wrinkles; and his trim frame. "You're looking fit as a fiddle," he said.

Tony's shrewd blue eyes studied Dirk as he released his friend's hand. "Fit as a fiddle? Seems I've heard that expression before, but not in Washington, D.C." He crossed the room and straddled a straight-backed chair. "As a matter of fact, Ellen's Tennessee relatives use it." He reached into his shirt pocket and pulled out a pipe. Tamping tobacco into the bowl, he said casually, "I don't suppose you met Dr. Ellen Stanford?"

"I thought you came here to tell me a fish story." Dirk also straddled a chair, facing his longtime friend.

"Why don't you tell me a fish story?" Tony took a long draw on his pipe. "How was fishing in the mountains?"

"They weren't biting."

"Is that a fact?" Tony puffed contentedly on his pipe and looked around the room. His gaze focused on the tattered bear on the bedside table. It had been the first thing he had noticed when he walked into the room. "You must be losing your touch, friend, to spend all summer and not catch a thing." He swung his gaze back to Dirk.

Dirk chuckled. "You don't miss a thing, do you?"

"Never have. Never intend to." Tony took another draw on his pipe. "What the hell are you doing with Ellen's stuffed bear?"

"You've met him?" Dirk glanced at Ellen's childhood companion.

"Damn right. I met Ellen Stanford the day she

moved to Beech Mountain. Helped her move. She's a hell of a woman."

"You'll get no argument from me on that point." Dirk willed himself to remain relaxed in his chair. All this talk of Ellen was heightening his unrest. With Tony here, talking of Beech Mountain and Pooh Bear, her presence in the room was almost a palpable thing. He could hear her laughter, see the moonlight on her flaming hair, feel the warmth of her skin. It might have been only last night since he'd seen her, instead of last week.

Tony nodded toward the bear. "That's an important part of Ellen's past. She wouldn't have parted with it unless she had a good reason." His blue eyes seemed to pierce through Dirk's very soul.

"You always did have the tenacity of a bulldog," Dirk said.

"Where my friends are concerned," Tony agreed. "What happened on that mountain—besides you not catching any fish?"

"I met Ellen the first day. Rocinante's radiator went dry in front of the compound." Talking about it was easier than Dirk had imagined. As he looked at his friend he reflected that perhaps he needed to confide in someone. Perhaps talking about Ellen would make losing her easier to bear.

Tony laughed. "A convenient ploy, if I ever heard one. Are you sure you didn't already know about the gorgeous doctor and plan it that way?"

"If I had known about the gorgeous doctor and what she would do to me, I would have run down that mountain and never looked back. She's more dangerous than the Mafia."

"Ah-ha. She got to you, did she?"

"Damn right." Dirk gazed into the empty space behind Tony's head, his eyes focused backward in time. "Damn right," he repeated softly, almost to himself, although he didn't believe it for a minute. His affair with Ellen was an experience that he wouldn't trade for a lifetime of contented solitude. "I made the mistake of falling in love."

"Then where the hell is Ellen?" Tony exploded. "What are you doing in D.C. with nothing but a raggedy teddy bear?"

Dirk's jaw clenched. "Don't you think I'd give all the gold in Fort Knox to have her here with me? Dammit, Tony, you know why she's not here."

"No. Tell me."

"What kind of life would any woman have with me?" He sprang from his chair and began to pace the room restlessly. "Never knowing where I am and whether I'll return." He swung around and glared fiercely at his friend. "Not to mention her work. She's committed to her research on Beech Mountain."

"Did you ever think of becoming a lawyer?" Tony asked dryly. "You almost convinced me."

Dirk smiled, thinking of Uncle Vester and Aunt Lollie. "I was a lawyer once."

"What?"

"Never mind." He propped one leg on a chair and looked down at Tony. "There's too much risk, Tony."

"Love is always a risk, Dirk." Removing his pipe, Tony held the bowl and pointed the stem for emphasis. "You're afraid."

"I fear nothing."

"Nothing except forming a bond that may not last." He jabbed the pipe in the air as he talked. "You're afraid to love, Dirk; afraid it will be snatched away just as it was in your childhood. It's time to put orphanages behind you and put down roots."

"That's pretty heavy stuff for an old gadabout

bachelor," Dirk said, grinning. But he felt a peculiar twinge, as if Tony had pinched a nerve of truth.

"We old gadabouts see more than you think we do." Tony blew a smoke ring into the air and squinted up at it. "Have you forgotten the story you told me?"

"In Spain?"

He smiled. "You do remember!"

Dirk's own smile grew thin at the edges. "I was about three sheets to the wind. Anyhow, that has nothing to do with Ellen." But Tony had pried open the door to his past, and the childhood memory came flooding back. He had been eight years old and a foster home had finally been found for him. For the first time in his life he had parents—Sam Dryden, a logger from Maine, and his stalwart wife, Erma. During the six months he was with them, he had felt a growing sense of love and security. And then bad things had started to happen. Sam was crippled in a logging accident and lost his job. Erma's health began to fail. As they struggled to cope with life, the little orphan boy became a liability, another mouth to feed. The family bonding was lost in tension and frustration. Finally survival dictated giving up the foster son. When he was sent back to the orphanage, he had believed that it was all somehow his fault. It was a feeling that stayed with him for years, and it had solidified his belief that love didn't last.

His face twisted with remembered pain. "That was a long time ago, Tony."

"But not so long ago that it can't play hell with your future." Tony took a thoughtful draw on his pipe. "It's time to make peace with the past, Dirk. You're not a mischievous little boy being shuffled off to another orphanage. You're not that little kid anymore who cried because he couldn't have a dog and kept a stiff upper lip when he was shipped away from his friends. Love is waiting on Beech Mountain. Go back and grab it."

"Your armchair psychology won't work with me."

Tony smiled. "Why don't we continue this discussion over a bottle of wine and a mess of fish?"

Dirk clapped his friend on the shoulder. "Done."

Dirk reached over the bedside table and picked up Ellen's tattered bear. The room was empty except for the two of them, but Tony's presence could still be felt in the aroma of pipe tobacco that hung in the air.

He traced the bear's permanent grin with one finger. "He could be right, you know." He set the bear back on the table and opened the top drawer. The folded paper rattled as he lifted it toward the light and opened it. There was no need to read the words again, he thought. He knew them by heart. From the time he had left Ellen beside Gigi's summer enclosure and found the bear on the backseat of his car, the words in that note had been emblazoned on his mind:

> Dirk,
>   Since I can't come with you, I'm sending a good friend to take my place. Pooh Bear is tattered from an overdose of loving, and he doesn't talk much, but he is still a good listener. Perhaps he can even fill the lonesome places in your heart.
>   Ellen

He studied the paper for a long time, then he began to smile. It was a slow smile that started at the corner of his mouth and spread upward to his eyes. By the time he had carefully refolded the note and put it in the drawer, his whole face was alight with the smile of discovery.

"I don't know which one is worse, you or Gigi," Ruth Ann grumbled to Ellen. "Both of you have been moping around here for two weeks."

Ellen carefully placed her pencil on top of her notes. It seemed that she did everything with care these days, as if any hurried movement would cause her to shatter. "Is this going to be a conference or a lecture?" she asked.

"It's time for a lecture." Ruth Ann patted her Mamie Eisenhower bangs although they needed no attention. "Either forget about that man or go after him."

"Go after him?"

"You heard me. Go after him. If you ask me, he's nothing but trouble." She paused and gave Ellen a sly smile. "Although I must say that he had his good points, one of them being his kindness to Gigi. Not every man is kind to animals. That shows a good heart."

Ellen pressed her hands to her temples as if she were trying to push Dirk from her mind. But it didn't work. Nothing worked. She would still feel his presence on this mountain, she decided, whether he stayed away two weeks or two months or two years. When Dirk had left in Rocinante, he had carried more than Pooh Bear: He had carried her heart.

She shoved her chair aside and stood up. "Of course, he has a good heart," she all but yelled. "I couldn't love a man who didn't. But he's gone. The affair is over and done with." She paced the small conference room as she talked. "Every affair has its rules, Ruth Ann. We played by the rules." She jerked her chair back to the table and sat down.

"You've always played by the rules, haven't you?" Ruth Ann asked quietly.

"What do you mean?"

"I mean that you've prided yourself on being a career woman, different from all the other Stanford women, and yet every year you return to Tennessee. You go in search of those very rules that you tell yourself you've left behind."

"If you're talking about marriage and preserving the family name, you can forget it. That was never important to me until I met Dirk, and now he's gone. Whether I'm bound by the codes of my ancestors is a moot point."

"I look like a fine one to talk, Ellen, with my sad spinster shoes and my narrow spinster ways, but there are two things I know: You can never escape your past and you can never escape love. I know; I tried."

Ellen covered Ruth Ann's hands in quick sympathy. "I didn't know."

"It was a long time ago. The details don't matter now. The important thing is that I see you making the same mistakes I did. You have that same damn stiff-necked pride, that abide-by-the-rules-if-it-kills-you attitude that made me the old sourpuss that I am."

Ellen protested. "You're not—"

"Yes, I am. An old tight-lipped crow who saw Dirk as a threat to the secure, safe life we have on this mountain. But I also have a heart, dried up as it may be." She gave a bitter laugh. "I love you, Ellen, and I don't like to see you hurting. If you love Dirk, go after him." She fiddled with her glasses and patted her hair to cover the sudden moisture in her eyes. "There. I've had my say."

"Thank you, Ruth Ann, for caring." Ellen patted the wrinkled hand. "Dirk's going was not my idea; it was his. Commitment has to work both ways. Besides, I don't even know where he is. I couldn't go after him if I wanted to." She reached blindly for her notes. "Let's get on with this conference."

"I'm ready when you are. But don't you think you'd better put down that banana and pick up your notebook?"

Ellen stared at the piece of fruit in her hands. "One of us needs a vacation," she said.

First the notes began to arrive. *Thinking of you. Dirk.* Postmarked Washington, D.C. *This city has no grapes.* No signature, just a New York City postmark. *A rose for remembrance.* Again no signature. A West German postmark and an envelope full of dried rose petals. Ellen's hopes soared.

And then her friends began acting funny. Tony paid an unexpected visit at the same time that Rachelle appeared at the compound with a cat-swallowed-the-canary grin.

Ellen looked up to see them both standing in her office doorway. "Well, hello, you two. What a pleasant surprise."

"Just popped in to see how the work's coming," Tony said. "That's all you do lately. Work."

"Me, too," Rachelle chimed in. "Just popped in, I mean. I'm afraid you're working too hard. It's about time for you to take a vacation."

Ellen propped her hands on her hips. "What is this? A conspiracy? I took a vacation early this summer."

"A trip to a family reunion is not a vacation,"

Rachelle said. "I mean a *real* vacation. Somewhere like Tahiti or Barbados or the Yukon."

"The Yukon!" Ellen laughed.

"The fishing's good up there," Tony said.

"I don't fish." Ellen removed her lab coat and hung it carefully on the coatrack. "All right, you two. What's going on?"

"Nothing," Rachelle said.

"Not a thing," Tony said.

Ellen didn't believe either one of them. "Since you're both here, why don't we have a cup of tea?" She gave them a beautiful smile. Perhaps she could coax it out of them over the teapot.

"What a great idea," Tony said.

"Super," Rachelle said. "You make the most fabulous tea."

Ellen laughed again. Even for Rachelle, that remark was out of character. "Tea is tea. Since when has mine been wonderful?" She poured fresh water into her teapot and plugged it in.

Rachelle shrugged. "You know me. Everything is wonderful these days. You should see the new ski instructor who's come to town. He has the most fabulous biceps this side of a Mr. America pageant. And those lips! Lord, you should see his lips." Rachelle sat down abruptly. "By the way, have you heard from Dirk?"

Was the question idle curiosity or previous knowledge? Ellen wondered. "I've had a note or two." She saw the look Tony and Rachelle exchanged. Pretending not to notice, she dropped teabags into three stoneware cups and poured the hot water. "One lump or two?" she asked Rachelle.

"The Yukon is probably nice this time of year," Rachelle said, overlooking the question of sugar.

"Great fishing," Tony said. "Beautiful scenery. Snow-capped mountains and rivers. A great place to go on vacation." He pulled up a chair beside Rachelle. "What did he say?"

Ellen dumped sugar into their teacups and pretended ignorance. "Who?"

"Dirk." Tony and Rachelle said the name simultaneously.

"When?" Ellen was beginning to enjoy watching the significant glances they were exchanging.

"In the notes," Rachelle prodded.

"Oh, this and that." Ellen stirred her tea. She could be maddening when she wanted to, and she decided this was the time to exercise that ability.

"Ruth Ann could fill in for you, you know," Rachelle said.

"Fill in for what?" Ellen asked.

"In case you decide to take a vacation," Tony said. "I could pop in every now and then to see that everything is all right. I'll still be in Dir—" He stopped and corrected himself in midsentence. "I'll be in my cabin."

Ellen lowered her cup carefully. It was a miracle that she didn't pour the whole scalding brew down the front of her dress. "What did you say?" she asked Tony.

"I'll pop in—"

"No. After that." She stared at him. "You said that you would *still* be in *Dirk's* cabin."

Tony took a great interest in his neglected tea. He stared into its murky depths for a full half minute, trying to think of a suitable reply.

Rachelle jumped into the conversational void. "That just shows how much you need a vacation. You've started hearing things."

Ellen suppressed a giggle as Tony gave Rachelle a thank-goodness-for-lying-friends look. They were definitely up to something, she decided, but they would never admit it. She decided to give them a break. "Your tea's getting cold."

Her conspiring friends grabbed their teacups as if they were lifeboats in a storm at sea.

"I've never seen Beech Mountain look so gorgeous this time of year," Rachelle said.

"Yes," Tony agreed, "the weather's beautiful."

Ellen smiled. She knew a conversational dead-end when she heard it. "Let's talk about the weather," she said, and figured their combined sigh of relief could be heard halfway down Beech Mountain.

The letters continued to come. They were all unsigned and all postmarked from various cities in West Germany. *The chicken coop here is stale compared to the one in Banner Elk.* That one made her laugh. *I never see red hair in the moonlight that I don't think of you.* That one made her cry. *Eggs have lost their savor.* That one put a zing into her step for the rest of the day.

She carefully folded each letter and put it in the top drawer of her dresser. At the end of each day she would get them all out and reread them. She was alternately elated and saddened that Dirk had broken all the rules. Her elation stemmed from hope and her sadness stemmed from the reminders. There should be no reminders of dead summer affairs, she thought. Letters only prolonged the agony of forgetting.

As the night sounds of September seeped through her window, Ellen thought of burning the letters, destroying all tangible evidence of Dirk's existence. Instead she smoothed them with her hands and tenderly shut them into the drawer. Be fair, she chided herself. You gave him Pooh Bear, hoping that it would be a constant reminder of you. It's all evidence. Evidence not of a dead affair but of a lasting love, a love that transcends time and distance.

It was a long time before she slept, and when she did, her dreams were haunted by Dirk.

A commotion outside the compound woke her. Ellen peered at her clock. Six A.M. Good Lord, she moaned to herself. Had Gigi run away again? She stumbled out of bed and into her robe. Without bothering to find her slippers, she raced down the hall and around the corner to her office. And then she heard them. Her bare feet skidded to a stop, and a wide grin split her face.

"Shhh, you silly old poop," a woman said. "You'll wake them all up."

"Shoot," a man replied. "Back home folks have been up and already done an hour's plowing."

Ellen ran out the door and down the porch steps. "Uncle Vester! Aunt Lollie!" She pulled them into her arms for a bear hug, then stood back to look at their dear faces. She knew that this was harvest time in Lawrence County. For Uncle Vester to leave his farm in September was almost unheard of. "What in the world brings you to Beech Mountain this time of year?" she asked.

Aunt Lollie winked at Uncle Vester and took charge of the situation. "There's a little nip in the mountain air, dear. Why don't we go inside while Vester unloads the bags?" Putting her arm around Ellen's waist, she led her inside. "My, my. What a trip. I thought that old pickup truck would never make it up this mountain. I don't know how Vester plans to get plumb out to Las Vegas in that old rattletrap when it will barely go from Tennessee to

North Carolina." She swung her head from side to side as she talked, her lively eyes taking in everything. "This is a right nice little place, dear. Put up a few gingham curtains and stick some gingerbread in the oven and it would be right homey." She nodded her head in satisfaction. "A nice little place to raise a family."

Ellen's heart sank down to her toes. She had to tell them, she thought. Now there was no waiting until next year's reunion. They were on the mountain, assessing the compound, still believing she was going to marry Dirk. She couldn't continue the deception any longer. "Sit down, Aunt Lollie," she said, indicating a chair beside the kitchen table. "I'll start a pot of coffee and then we'll talk."

Aunt Lollie smiled and patted Ellen's cheek. "I've been sittin' for two hundred miles. I'll put on the coffee while you go and spiffy up."

Ellen laughed. "I'll have to disappoint you, Aunt Lollie. My work clothes aren't what you'd call spiffy, but then nobody's around to see except Ruth Ann and Gigi."

"You never know." Aunt Lollie's serene face was wreathed in smiles. "Here's Vester. Now scoot along, dear, while I unwrap that gingerbread I brought."

Ellen obeyed without further argument. Obeying Aunt Lollie was a habit not easily broken. It also gave her a brief reprieve. As she hurried down the hall to her bedroom, she decided that she would tell them as soon as she returned to the kitchen.

Ruth Ann stuck her head around her door as Ellen whizzed by. "Company?"

"My Aunt Lollie and Uncle Vester," Ellen said. "Aunt Lollie sent me to dress."

"Two of my favorite people. I'll go to the kitchen and visit with them while you dress."

As Ellen walked on toward her room she reflected that Ruth Ann hadn't looked very surprised. What in the world was going on? she wondered. In spite of having told Aunt Lollie that she didn't wear spiffy clothes to work in, Ellen dressed with unusual care. The bright yellow aviator-style jump suit with front zipper emphasized her figure and enhanced her red hair.

She reached to the dresser for her wristwatch and, on impulse, opened the top drawer and took out the stack of letters. Closing her eyes, she recalled all the words Dirk had written. Although the words were few, each one had a special significance. They cataloged the affair, capturing it forever on folded pieces of paper.

She touched the letters to her lips before returning them to the drawer. "Good-bye, Dirk," she whispered. "It's too bad that I have to take you out of my life forever."

Squaring her shoulders with determination, she started back to the kitchen to set the record straight about her fake fiancé.

Aunt Lollie looked up from the pan of steaming hot gingerbread that she was removing from the oven. "My, my. You look like a daffodil."

Ellen had to grip the back of a chair. Aunt Lollie couldn't have known that Dirk had once told her the same thing. "That—" The word came out a croak, and she had to start again. "That gingerbread smells delicious."

"Nobody makes it like Lollie." Uncle Vester put his arm around Ellen's shoulder. "Come sit by me, young'un. You're prettier than a speckled pup in the sunshine. I bet when that bridegroom sees you, he'll sit up and beg." He slapped his leg and laughed delightedly at his own humor.

The color drained from Ellen's face. She couldn't

let this deception go on another minute. "There's something I have to tell both of you."

"I think it had better wait awhile, dear," Aunt Lollie said. "There's a man on a white horse in your front yard."

Ellen flew to the window. "Dirk!" she shouted. He was sitting atop White Fire, bronzed and smiling. She swung her gaze back to the kitchen. "You knew." She was laughing and crying at the same time. "All this time you knew."

"Are you going to keep that young feller waitin'?" Uncle Vester asked.

"Do you know how much I love you?" she said to her relatives before she bolted from the kitchen.

Her feet took wings as she ran across the yard toward Dirk. He bent down and scooped her into his arms. Three interested pairs of eyes watched from the kitchen window as the reunited lovers joined in a passionate kiss.

"Just like in the movies," Aunt Lollie said.

"Mark my words. This mountain will soon be crawlin' with kids," Uncle Vester said.

"I feel the winds of change," Ruth Ann said.

Ellen hooked her leg over the saddlehorn and settled herself more comfortably against Dirk's shoulder. "It's a wonder you didn't kill yourself trying to ride this stallion," she said.

"You're worth the risk." His face wore the old devil-may-care smile, the same one he had worn when she first saw him. "Besides, have you ever known a prince who rode a nag like Annie?"

She gazed deep into his eyes. "Are you my prince?"

His eyes crinkled at the corners when he smiled. "Why don't you ask Pooh Bear?" He pulled the ragged bear from the saddlebag.

"Oh, Dirk." She touched the bear's button eye. "You kept him."

"I kept him, love. Believe it or not, this feisty little bear is now a world traveler. I carried him all over Germany. He told me all your secrets."

"Including the one about me waiting for a prince?"

"Yes, love. Including that one." He brushed his lips against her hair. "I want to be your prince. I've come back to ride off into the sunset with you if you'll have me."

"It's the wrong time of day," she teased. She could hardly believe everything that was happening. In spite of the letters, in spite of her friends' odd behavior, in spite of Aunt Lollie and Uncle Vester and White Fire, she had to have more evidence that Dirk was back in her life to stay.

"When was there ever a wrong time of day for us?" he asked, then nudged White Fire with his heels. The stallion cantered up the mountain.

Ellen exulted in the feel of wind on her cheeks and Dirk holding her tight. So many questions to ask, she thought, so many things to say. But they would wait. She was with the man she loved, and right now nothing else mattered.

She felt the thunder of hooves under her and the thunder of Dirk's heart behind her as they plunged up the mountain. She scarcely noticed the wild flowers that beribboned the mountains in splashes of color as they hastened toward Tony's cabin.

Dirk reined in under the pine trees. "We're home."

Ellen half turned in the saddle. "What will Tony think if we barge in like this?"

"Tony is in a condominium in Banner Elk. I bought this place when he came to Washington." He slid from the horse and helped her down. "I think you'll like that stable I had built out back for White Fire."

She stood on top of Beech Mountain with the early-morning sun warming her back and looked up at Dirk. A long time ago her heart had said yes to this man, perhaps even that first day on her front porch at the compound. In time she would learn all the hows and whys of his return, but for now she would rejoice in his presence.

Her arms slipped around his neck. "You did all this," she asked softly, "without telling me?" She touched the pulse point of his throat with her lips.

"Well, ma'am, I saw this wonderful opportunity, and I grabbed it." He smiled down at her as he affected a Southern drawl and repeated the words he had used that day at the beginning of summer, the day he had become her fiancé.

She cupped his face in her hands. "My prince on a white charger, would you mind carrying Opportunity inside? I think I hear a bunch of grapes calling our names."

Without another word he picked her up and carried her across the threshold of their new home in the mountains. By the time they had reached the brass bed, their clothes were strewn in an erratic path on the floor. The mattress creaked a welcome, and the songbirds outside the window celebrated the occasion with joyous carols.

"I've waited all my life for this," Dirk whispered against the satin skin of her neck. "I've waited all my life to say these words." He lifted his head and looked into her eyes.

"I'm listening, Dirk." She tenderly brushed a lock of tousled dark hair off his forehead.

"I love you, Dr. Ellen Stanford. I want to spend the rest of my life with you. I want you to be my lover and my wife. I want you to be my home and my hearth. I want you to be my present and my future."

"I promise to be those things and more." Their eyes locked as she pledged her vows. "I promise to fill all the lonesome places of your heart."

And then, before the wedding and the ring and the minister, their vows were sealed there on the brass bed with the sun streaming through the sky-light as witness.

Afterward they lay in a tangled heap of content-ment. Dirk lifted a strand of flaming hair and let it drift through his fingers. "Can you live with my career, love?"

Ellen thought for a moment. She had a vague idea what that meant—danger, uncertainty, sepa-ration, but she had to know more. "Tell me about your career, Dirk. Just how dangerous is it?"

"Movies and spy novels have overplayed the dan-ger, but it does exist. When I do fieldwork, I'm always armed and there's always a possibility that I won't return." His arms tightened around her. "There's also a slight chance of retaliatory action against my family."

She lay very still, trying not to let his words strike cold terror in her heart. Loving this man meant accepting all of him, Ellen told herself. "Tell me about the fieldwork," she said softly.

"Sometimes my assignments are as simple as diplomatic relations. I'll be just a phone call away, as those crazy ads say. Other times you will know neither the nature of the assignment nor the place. I could be gone days or even weeks without your hearing from me. I take only three or four field assignments a year. Between assignments I have extended leaves—six to eight weeks. The rest of the time I would work out of Washington and com-mute on weekends." He raised himself on an elbow so he could look down into her face. "I know it's a heavy burden to ask any woman to share, but I have enough confidence in my own abilities to believe that I can minimize the danger and the uncertainty. Can you accept that, Ellen?"

She looked into his eyes. "It's not an easy thing to accept, but one hour as your wife is worth the risk." She reached up to smooth the laugh lines that fanned out from his eyes. "I trust you, Dirk, and I accept you—all of you." Turning her face into his neck, she nuzzled close. "Home will be a haven, and each day we spend together will be magic." She nipped his skin. It was time to move to a less somber topic. "Can you live with my career?"

He laughed. "Does that mean I have to live on bananas and cauliflower and give Gigi regular driving lessons?"

"Only the driving lessons," she teased.

"I'd rather face a firing squad."

She lazily walked her fingertips through the dark hair on his chest. "Dirk?"

"Mmm?"

"How long have you known that you would come back and when did you do all this?"

He ran his tongue around the rim of her ear. "This?"

"No." She laughed, swinging her arm to encompass the cabin. "This. White Fire. Aunt Lollie and Uncle Vester."

He rolled on top of her, bracing most of his weight on his arms. "That's what I get for being in love with a scientist. Always probing for answers." His black eyes were sparkling with all the joy he was feeling. "Tony came to see me after he returned from his fishing trip. I knew before he left that I would come back. I was leaving on field assignment, so he had the stables built and brought

White Fire here. Rachelle helped with the arrangements."

"I knew those two were up to something."

"As soon as I returned from Germany, I went to see Uncle Vester and Aunt Lollie."

"You told them the whole story?"

He laughed. "No, but I told them the truth—that I loved you, had loved you from the first moment I saw you, and that we were going to be married on this mountain."

She rolled her eyes in mock horror. "Such a deceitful pair we are!"

"I would say that we were made for each other." He bent down and traced her eyes with the tip of his tongue. "Wouldn't you?"

"I don't know." She captured his face between her hands. "You'll have to convince me."

And he did.

Ellen looked out the window at the glorious day, her wedding day. Her hands caressed the slipper satin of her wedding dress. Nature was the best decorator in the world, she thought. The enclosed bower beside the lake would be flooded with sunshine and filled with the fragrance of wild roses.

She felt a tug on her wedding veil and turned from the window. Gigi was standing behind her, clutching her bridesmaid bouquet so hard that the flowers were wilting on broken stems.

Gigi pointed to her bare head, and then Ellen's veil.

Gigi want hat, she signed.

Rachelle and Ruth Ann burst through the bedroom door, panting. "We tried to get her to wear this," Rachelle said, holding up a garland of silk flowers, "but she refused."

"She's insisting on a 'pretty hat' like yours," Ruth Ann said. "Lord knows, it's bad enough that Dirk's taking you off to the Salinger cabin. Did he have to insist on having a gorilla for a bridesmaid?" Ruth Ann tried to preserve her image as a severe sourpuss, but she was smiling.

"You know full well that the cabin is only three miles away and is perfect for my work here." Ellen was smiling too. Nothing could spoil this glorious day. "Furthermore, we wouldn't dream of being married without Gigi. She's really the one who brought us together."

Rachelle faked a swoon on Ellen's bed. "I adore a good romance."

The gorilla tugged the veil again. *Gigi want fine hat.*

Ellen patted Gigi's head and said, signing, "Ellen will get you a hat. Fine hat for fine animal gorilla."

"And how do you propose to do that?" Ruth Ann asked. "The wedding's only an hour away and there are no stores open today anyhow."

"You don't know my Aunt Lollie." Ellen walked into the hallway and called, "Aunt Lollie, can you come in here a minute."

Aunt Lollie poked her head out of the kitchen. "I'll be right there, dear." She drifted into the bedroom, bringing with her the pungent aroma of cinnamon and cloves. "I do declare, I believe your Uncle Vester is going to eat every single one of those Italian bowknots before the reception."

"Gigi wants to wear a veil, Aunt Lollie," Ellen said.

"Well, thread me a needle, dear, and fetch me a muslin sheet. Time's a-wastin'."

Twenty minutes later Gigi preened before the mirror in her makeshift wedding veil. *Fine hat,* she pronounced, and then looked at Ellen's satin pumps. Pointing to her feet, she signed, *Poor Gigi. No shoes. Gigi want fine shoes.*

Ruth Ann heaved a great sigh. "We've spoiled her rotten. Who ever heard of a gorilla in high heels?"

"Who ever heard of high heels big enough for a gorilla?" Rachelle asked.

"Vester brought extra shoes," Aunt Lollie volunteered.

"Yes, but are they fine?" Ellen said, laughing.

"Why don't we ask Gigi?" Aunt Lollie left the bedroom and returned with Uncle Vester's pride and joy, a pair of wingtip shoes, relics of his courting days. "It's a good thing that darling old poop has big feet," she said as she wedged the shoes onto Gigi's feet.

Gigi sat in the middle of the floor and held her feet up for inspection. She looked like a solemn sheikh as she turned her head with the muslin sheet from side to side and studied the shoes. Finally she smiled. *Fine shoes,* she signed. She rose to her feet and stood beside Ellen. *Gigi damn good pretty bride,* she signed.

Ruth Ann and Ellen exchanged startled glances.

"Who in the world taught her to cuss?" Ruth Ann asked.

"Can't you guess?" Ellen asked.

"Dirk," they said simultaneously.

"I think we'd better go before she decides she needs a dress," Rachelle suggested.

The unlikely wedding party climbed into Ellen's aging Buick and Uncle Vester's 1955 Chevrolet pickup truck and chugged up the mountain to meet the bridegroom. Dirk and Tony and the minister were waiting for them in the rose bower beside the lake.

The smile Dirk gave his bride rivaled the brilliance of the sun. As Ellen came to him across the rose-scented clearing, she looked deep into his eyes and saw a reaffirmation of the commitment they had already made. She saw the love and trust that would bind them together in spite of the time and distance that would sometimes separate them.

She reached out her hand, and there in nature's cathedral they became husband and wife, a promise for the future.

Epilogue

Dirk plucked a rose from an overhanging vine and let the petals drift onto Ellen's breasts. "I'm thinking of the Yukon," he said.

"Not again." Ellen pretended to be horrified. Her green eyes were alight with love and contentment as she looked up at her husband. "Every time we go to the Yukon, I come home pregnant."

He grinned wickedly. "That's the general idea." He bent down and retrieved a rose petal with his lips. "Besides, can you think of a better way to keep warm?"

"Blankets?" she teased.

He plucked another rose petal from her breast. "If we had one more baby, we'd have a quartet."

"I didn't know you could sing." She traced the strong line of his jaw with her fingertips. If she lived to be a hundred, she thought, she would never cease to find magic with this man.

"Who knows what I'll do since I'm retiring from fieldwork," he said. "Think of it, Ellen. With our own quartet we could become the singing Benedicts." Throwing back his head, he gave her a demonstration. His rendition of "The Old Gray Mare" was so terrible that even the squirrels in a nearby pine tree covered their ears.

Ellen laughed. "I don't think the Osmonds have anything to worry about." She sat up and shook the grass from her hair. "Help me find my clothes, Dirk, so we can go back and dress for the retirement party."

"Who's making the punch?"

"Gigi."

"That's what I was afraid of." He pulled her into his arms and lowered her back to the ground. Her hair made a scarlet fan on the grass. "I have a better idea, love. We can pretend this forest glade is the Yukon."

She felt a familiar rush of desire as she looked up into his laughing dark eyes. "Only if you promise one thing."

"Anything," he said as his lips sought her breasts.

"Promise you won't teach this baby to sing."

His reply was the first powerful thrust that erased everything else from their minds, and they set about making the fourth member of their quartet.

THE EDITOR'S CORNER

We've received the most glorious comments about **SUNSHINE AND SHADOW** from booksellers and reviewers who got advance reading copies of this wonderful novel by Sharon and Tom Curtis! "Pure magic" is what one bookseller called this powerfully evocative love story, and, indeed, "magic" seemed to be the key word in almost everyone's comments. But, as **SUNSHINE AND SHADOW** is on sale at the very minute you're reading this, I'm sure you'll want to get a copy and decide for yourself what is the most appropriate description. Enchanting? Joyous? Poignant? Tender? Touching? Sensuous and sensual? Utterly captivating? I'd vote for all those . . . along with "pure magic," of course, and a continuing string of glowing adjectives. You simply must not miss this exquisitely beautiful and heart-stoppingly exciting love story of two people from completely different backgrounds. Need I add that it is written as only the Curtises could write it?

TOO MANY HUSBANDS, LOVESWEPT #159, is by a delightful newcomer to the ranks of LOVE-SWEPT authors, Charlotte Hughes. In this charming, slightly wacky romance, beautiful, but hassled heroine Meri Kincaid finds herself with too many husbands, indeed. How, you ask, can Meri be out of jail . . . not even facing a longtime sentence for being in this spot? Well, she's not *really* a wife to the twelve grateful bachelors in her life. In a financial fix after the sudden death of her husband, Meri had turned to homemaking to support herself and her young daughter. Now she has her hands full running the homes—and the lives—of those men, so how can she take on yet another client? Enter

(continued)

Lucky Thirteen! He's Chet Ambrose, one handsome hunk of a sweet man who proposes they swap services. She will provide cleaning and cooking for him; he'll use his carpentry skills to prevent her ramshackle house from falling apart. Whew! Talk about falling . . . there are falling ladders (no black cats, though) and a whole lot of falling in love . . . and you'll find yourself falling under a spell as you read this warmhearted and exciting romance.

BEDSIDE MANNERS, LOVESWEPT #160 features more of Barbara Boswell's totally endearing and wonderfully quirky characters. Here, Dr. Case Flynn, whom you met in Barbara's first ever published romance, **LITTLE CONSEQUENCES,** is the hospital lothario. But that sexy devil more than meets his match in Dr. Sharla Shakarian who is not only luscious to look at but an outstanding pediatrician, and a wonderfully warm and wise woman. Case is definitely *not* the marrying kind—not with the parents he'd had! And Sharla's a family-centered lady, if there ever was one. Add to this basic conflict the dramas of the hospital they work in, their well-meaning families and friends, and most of all the raging hunger between them and you have one heck of a delectable romance from one heck of a talented author!

It will be a very long time before I forget the beauty of Fran Baker's first romance for us, **SEEING STARS,** LOVESWEPT #161. Just as Nick Monroe's laugh steals Dovie Brown's heart, so will it steal yours. And Dovie's sweet, but fierce need for love will make you ache for her, just as you ache because of the tragic consequences of an accident Nick had. When these two humorous, fiery, loving people overcome the obstacles that separate them,
(continued)

you'll find yourself cheering! Set in moutain country, **SEEING STARS** is rich in atmosphere and in the exploration of the differences that are only superficial when two hearts beat as one.

Now, sit back and enjoy some big chuckles and large guffaws with **SECRETS OF AUTUMN,** LOVESWEPT #162 by Joan Elliott Pickart. Autumn Stanton just couldn't resist using Graham Kimble in her research. Trying to prove that men respond to the superficial aspects of women, she masqueraded as dowdy Agatha, bright and capable, but definitely plain as ditchwater. Then she fell for Graham even as he seemed to fall for her. How could she have guessed that such a womanizer had sworn off bubbleheaded beauties and was determined to find a woman whose looks were nothing special? This is just the beginning of one of Joan's most delightful romps . . . spiced with tender emotion and inevitable fireworks!

We hope you'll enjoy all the books we're publishing next month as much as we enjoyed helping to bring them to you.

With every good wish,

Carolyn Nichols

Carolyn Nichols
   Editor
LOVESWEPT
Bantam Books, Inc.
666 Fifth Avenue
New York, NY 10103

His love for her is madness.
Her love for him is sin.

Sunshine
and
Shadow

by Sharon and Tom Curtis

COULD THEIR EXPLOSIVE LOVE BRIDGE THE CHASM BETWEEN TWO IMPOSSIBLY DIFFERENT WORLDS?

He thought there were no surprises left in the world ... but the sudden appearance of young Amish widow Susan Peachey was astonishing—and just the shock cynical Alan Wilde needed. She was a woman from another time, innocent, yet wise in ways he scarcely understood.

Irresistibly, Susan and Alan were drawn together to explore their wildly exotic differences. And soon they would discover something far greater—a rich emotional bond that transcended both of their worlds and linked them heart-to-heart ... until their need for each other became so overwhelming that there was no turning back. But would Susan have to sacrifice all she cherished for the uncertain joy of their forbidden love?

"Look for full details on how to win an authentic Amish quilt displaying the traditional 'Sunshine and Shadow' pattern in copies of SUNSHINE AND SHADOW or on displays at participating stores. No purchase necessary. Void where prohibited by law. Sweepstakes ends December 15, 1986."

Look for SUNSHINE AND SHADOW in your bookstore or use this coupon for ordering: